# Behold, He Scatters His Lightning

Shelly Lyons

Edited by Paula Nevins of Ember & Ink Author Services

Editing by Emily Haynes

Edited by Jacob Floyd

Cover by Christy Aldridge of Grim Poppy Designs

Formatting by Megan Nevins of Ember & Ink Author Services

*News clippings are from 1923 and earlier

# *Behold, He Scatters His Lightning*

## *By Shelly Lyons*

*. . . Behold, He scatters His lightning about Him*
*and covers the roots of the sea.*
*For by these He judges peoples;*
*He gives food in abundance.*
*He covers His hands with the lightning*
*and commands it to strike the mark.*
*Its crashing declares His presence . . .*
*—Job 36:30–33*

# George Fade III

The Glen Elder Sentinel.

GLEN ELDER, MITCHELL COUNTY, KANSAS, THURSDAY, JULY 16, 1908

### Struck by Lightning.

Last Monday evening during the storm here the Talkington family had a narrow escape from a bolt of lightning which struck the roof of the house, it being a metal roof the lightning glanced off and struck the telephone wire which led into the house. Mr. Talkington was seated near the door and close to the telephone and received quite a shock, the lightning burned his nose slightly and permeated his entire system. He says it was as close as he cares to have it get to him.

# Prologue

The wet heat of June lazed around like a drunk guy, and George Fade III was a guy who needed a drink. He couldn't, though. It made him vulnerable. He was back in the crosshairs of his enemy, after all, and lest he forget, its thunder rolled across the plains.

Seized by the inevitability of his demise, George twitched around on the prayer table, pinned under eight healing hands.

"It's spotted me! It knows I'm here!"

He should hide where it couldn't get to him, not laid out like a buffet in front of the big window. But Pastor Ed spoke with such passion, as if the entire congregation was in the room, George couldn't interrupt. So, he anchored his thoughts in the world of faith rather than that of a fire-spitting destroyer circling his tainted soul.

"Jesus, we come to You as a group to praise You, and beg You for Your continuous love, and ask that You come heal our ailing brother in Christ, Amen." Pastor Ed's voice boomed louder than George had expected and he cringed in its reverberations.

Pushing him more firmly onto the table, the pastor's helpers, a trio of sandy-haired, prairie-freckled fellows whose names George continued to mix up even after twenty-five years off and on in the same church, echoed their "Amens."

"God is our impenetrable shield. We take refuge in the Lord because He loves and cares for us, and so that we may receive His divine protection—"

A distant whip crack gave everyone a jolt. For a split second, the men's hands left George's body, and he sprang into a sitting position.

"Christ, it's not gonna work!"

"Hold on to your faith," Pastor Ed said in those gentle tones he used for the bereaved. "Let go of your doubts."

"A long time ago, I did things, Pastor. I cannot be forgiven!"

"Jesus forgives the sinners, George." Pastor Ed's big, warm fingers bore down on his skull. "Jesus, our savior, restore faith to your servant!" The edge of his onyx pinky ring dug into George's skin. "Remove fear and doubt from his heart by the power of Your Holy Spirit, and may You, Lord, be glorified through his life. Amen!"

At the pastor's look, the men removed their hands and shuffled over to Pastor Ed's shiny maple desk.

The eyes of his healers weighed heavy on George's back as he stood up, doused in sweat, heart banging against his ribs, and buttoned his denim jacket. Outside the big window clouds scudded across orange skies to the Smoky Hills. George felt every bit like the ant in the giant's shadow.

"We are embraced by the Lord's protection," Pastor Ed said. "Can you feel it, brothers?"

The other fellows said "Yes" and "Amen," but their

demeanors told George they did not, especially when lightning lit up the darkening sky and a couple of them gasped.

George's eyes flew to his digital watch. He pushed a button to start the timer.

"Why don't we go into the chapel?"

George shushed the pastor with his hand, listened until thunder clapped, then pressed the timer again. "Eleven point seven seconds. Divided by five is . . . two point four miles away."

"Don't give in to fear, George. Stay with faith. If we keep the Lord in our hearts—" Pastor Ed reached for him, but George was already out the door.

Through the hallway, across the altar, and down a long aisle flanked by empty pews, George decided he was alone in this after all, despite the clack of Pastor Ed's fancy boots behind him. Only one thing to do now, and that was to pray, and only one place to do it, and that was home. He shot through the vestibule and burst out the front doors into the purple dusk.

His stringy black hair whipped around as he shouldered through the gusts, pausing only when the auto-timer lit up the church's marquee, startling him.

LAMB OF GOD CONGREGATION

Sunday service 10 am. & Bible Study after

Wednesday service 6 pm.

Thursday Adult Bible Study 6 pm

*"Put on the full armor of God, so that you can stand against the schemes of the Devil."* Ephesians 6:13

*What kind of armor do I have?* HE PUZZLED, HOPPING into his F-150.

Pastor Ed hollered from the church doors: "George! There's more to do!"

"Don't let it see you, Pastor!"

A tendril of flame lashed the sky east over the Kanopolis Drive-In. Thunder arrived three seconds later. "Half mile. Oh, help me, Jesus." Hammering the accelerator, George screeched through the vast parking lot and was soon dough-nutting into a roundabout that spit him onto the road.

A monotone voice on the radio cautioned: ". . . *Winds are blowing at approximately sixty miles per hour . . .*"

In his rearview mirror, the storm swept across the prairie with the force of a freight train.

"*. . . Locations impacted include Ellsworth County and Barton County . . .*"

The landscape strobed white.

"*. . . Please take cover immediately. Avoid windows, or get to the lowest level of a sturdy building . . .*"

Radio static overwhelmed the voice. The *gh**zzzzzzzzzz**ht- gh**zzzzzzzzzz**ht* transformed into snarls of thunderclaps, and from this thunder emerged a deep, ragged voice.

*"George number three."*

George slapped the radio off. The black storm now fully cloaked the skies behind him, with occasional pulses in the shape of eyeball veins.

*"Number three. Coming for ya, coming for ya . . ."*

Guessing it didn't matter whether the radio was off or on, George loudly hummed "Amazing Grace" as he sifted through memories for some kind of goodness. He quickly found Gina, his little Gina, grown up now, Gina who had inherited his nose and overbite, and his drinking habits—

Lovely Gina, who'd started calling him last year because of one of the Twelve Steps. The thought of seeing her again brought his foot down on the accelerator.

*"I'll take you again, number three."*

Thunder clapped its gigantic cosmic hands and ripped apart the sky.

"In the name of Jesus Christ, leave me alone!"

Insane laughter filled the cab.

George burst into a weeping so hard his windshield wipers were for shit. In minutes, he skidded a right turn into his long, dirt driveway. A lightning bolt missed the truck by inches but sent his mailbox sizzling off its post. Roof shingles flew past; several grazed the windshield.

The truck had barely stopped before George threw himself out and dashed up the stairs to his door, repeating, "Do not be afraid, do not be discouraged, for the Lord your God will be with you wherever you go!"

Porch chimes shrieked in the hefty gusts. George's back tingled as the darkness rampaged up the driveway. He tore off his jacket. Pawed at his keychain. Found the door key! Then dropped the whole damn key ring! "Christ, help me! Fucking help me!" His arm hairs sizzled to curly stumps. "Jesus, God!" With shaky hands he scooped up the keys and shoved the proper one into the lock. Only then did he risk a look back—in the same moment, a cloud-to-ground bolt melted the truck's paint and tires.

George stumbled inside, reached for the light switch, then stopped himself. Mustn't touch anything electrical! He hunkered in the middle of his living room, squatting with arms around his knees. Lightning haunted every window, searching for a way inside. He trembled and tried not to breathe and tried to catch his breath and prayed it would not hear him.

Through it all, he clung to the hope that Jesus would intervene, especially when Gina's image returned to him. The scowl she sometimes wore during their video calls gave way to an easy smile, so bright and unfiltered, forgiving all his weaknesses and failures. She nodded at the rotary phone on the TV tray by his recliner.

The first ring startled him. The second ring was proof that the first ring happened. And the third filled him with joy. This could only be Gina, his Gina, Gina Ballerina, who God must've compelled to call him! He rushed to the phone, spirits swelling. "Hello, Gina?"

The receiver popped as electricity zipped through its lines. George's body stiffened. Flames exploded from his chest. His eyes spun back as he succumbed to the sting of the white light shaking him into oblivion.

"Dad?" said Gina. "Hello? Dad? Are you fucking with me?"

A scream, a demented giggle, a sigh, and then George Fade III was gone.

"Dad? Dad! DAD!"

# Gina Fade Returns

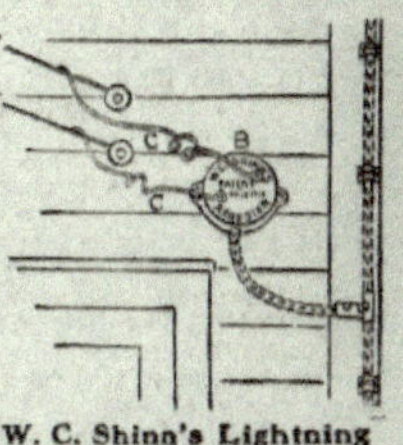

# Chapter One

Traveling straight from an outpatient group home to her dead father's farmhouse in the middle of Bumfuck Nowhere, Kansas raised quite a few sober counselor eyebrows. But Gina had no choice. As the only child of George Fade III, whose name she kept despite her parents' divorce and years of silence between them, she was his sole beneficiary and therefore needed to lay claim.

It's what she told herself, anyway.

She forgot how the place looked, and so entertained visions of a quaint farmhouse with good bones she could fix up. A little paint, new furniture, rustic curtains, hanging plants, sage-green tile in the bathroom, *et voila!* Farmhouse chic she'd rent to Kansas City professionals who craved an authentic prairie experience.

Mom's last words as Gina left for the airport were, "Don't pick up any hitchhikers." So, naturally, when Gina pulled her rental Hyundai into a travel stop west of Lawrence, Kansas for some munchies, she offered a ride to Yannick Kessler, a young German backpacker drifting through America. At thirty, Gina remained a contrary teenager defying expectations. Just cuz. Which was as far as she could ever explain it in therapy.

Yannick deposited his gear in the back seat and belted up. As Gina started the car, he brandished a couple of airplane-sized Jack Daniel's bottles and offered her one.

Her throat moistened at the sight of the dark amber liquid. "Um. No drinking in my car, sorry."

"Have I done bad?"

"No. I can't be around alcohol, so . . ."

"Should I place them in the trunk?"

"No. It's fine. Just don't open them."

"Yes, miss."

She patted his be-denimed knee, culminating in a few suggestive finger swirls. "Thank you. I used to be a real fuckup. Kind of still am."

As the city gave way to the flat greenish-brown horizons, they listened to auto-tuned pop ditties on a preset and took stabs at conversation. She tried making her graphic design work seem important, leaving out the part where her drinking had cost her all her clients.

Yep. She was downright charming, despite a steady thrum of apprehension at the prospect of going to Dad's place.

Yannick boasted about his darkwave band in Leipzig, called Puppenfabrik. "We explore thematic concepts of darkness. Once you have seen it, the darkness sees you."

She nodded, picturing him shirtless in eyeliner and leather pants.

"You should be up by the Great Lakes, or down in New Orleans." She'd been to neither area. "God knows why you'd come here, unless—were you a huge *Supernatural* fan?"

"I go where the rides take me," he replied with the gravitas of a world-weary nomad. His pretentiousness stoked the part of her that used to love discussing philosophy before getting railed. She'd put money on there being a dog-eared copy of *On the Road* buried deep in his backpack.

It didn't take long before Gina, despite two months on the wagon and a few hundred hours of talk therapy, fell back to impulsive behaviors of yore.

Yannick asked to pull over so he could take her picture, "to immortalize the beautiful lady in the open space with only the sky and clouds." Minutes later, she stood roadside with her arms outstretched like "Hey from America!" When he showed her the pictures for her approval, she leaned in for a closer look, and his hand brushed her breast. Game on. For six sweaty, grunting minutes behind a roadside haystack, Gina's mind emptied of past regrets and fears of the yet-to-come. She didn't care if she died face-first in the hay. Only lunatic pleasure mattered in this moment.

On their stroll back to the car, Yannick pointed at a dark spot on the horizon. "Darkness brings the storm."

"At least we're not driving into it."

Minutes later, she gunned the car toward that very darkness, explaining the game of Chicken to him as he clutched the passenger seat's grab handle. Of course, she'd turn south before the storm, but figured sex and fear would ensure he'd take home a story about the wild broad who drove straight into a storm and fucked him by a haystack. Maybe he'd write a song about her for Puppenfabrik. *There should be a Moog synthesizer involved,* she decided. *Lots of Moog. That's me. Raw, analog future magic.*

Gina and her nervous passenger entered a downtown Ellsworth blanketed with clouds. She gave Yannik a sloppy kiss, then whispered into his ear, "Think of me when you're waiting at the side of a lonely road."

He promised to find her when his band came to tour. Her last sight of him was a goodbye wave before he disappeared into a tourist saloon with a longhorn statue on its roof.

Gina dismissed fears of chlamydia, or worse, as she got on Highway 14 south. Storm clouds in her rearview. Nine miles to Dad's place, and twenty-three years since she saw it last.

# Chapter Two

GPS announced her destination was coming up on the right. A heavy fog settled in Gina's stomach. If only she could blink herself into another reality. She'd give anything to sit alongside the Champs-Élysées sipping wine and people watching right now. Or even enjoying a Diet Coke in the Burbank Mall food court.

Until this moment, she'd recognized nothing in this environment—just a thin road fringed by prairie grass and sporadic houses set far off the road. Now a déjà vu capered through her at the sight of her dad's dirt driveway. The broken mailbox was a concern she'd have to deal with later.

Massive red mulberry trees hampered her view of the house, with only its pointed roof visible behind them. Dozens of rusty old cars sat parked near the barn. The barn. Shit. She'd blanked out its image all these years. For good reason. It always seemed to glower at her, although Gina tended to anthropomorphize everything, which used to make throwing away empty bottles of whiskey difficult. "You eased me into a blackout sir. You will be missed."

She steered left and passed dozens of newer cars, cars

too new to be a part of Dad's collection. *Crap. People are inside the house.*

At this point, the house revealed itself, ending all her greedy speculation with a whimper. Before her loomed a tottering relic the Big Bad Wolf could blow down with a mere sneeze. Her only path to income would be Airbnb-ing this bitch to goth couples with expendable incomes. They could listen to 16 Horsepower while freaking out about the relentless winds. Niche as shit.

A Ford truck parked closest to the porch looked as though someone had driven it across the sun. She didn't want to imagine what happened, but knew it belonged to Dad.

The wind flapped up her hoodie as she got out to for a closer look at her childhood home. Same big porch covered by an old wood awning, same slender house with its pitched roof, same collection of smallish windows everywhere, which Little-Gina once imagined were the eyes of a friendly spider. She'd assign each eye new things to surveil every few weeks.

A nagging memory teased but didn't reveal itself. Her alcoholism had exposed the fragility of her recollections, playing as old eight-reel movies on dirty walls. Through one of its eyes, she'd seen something, and then a dust settled, dissipating the fragment before she understood what it was.

*Try not to cry today*, she admonished herself as she strapped on her cross-body purse and duffel bag. *Don't you dare cry.*

A curlicue of smoke wafted to her from the stairs, where a man sat smoking a cigarette.

"I assume this is George Fade's house?" Her shadow fell over him.

"Yup. The viewing started an hour ago."

She eyed his oatmeal-colored suit, honey-blond hair, and the splash of freckles on his cheeks. A beige man.

"Nobody told me about a viewing. Who's hosting?"

"Lamb of God Assembly." He blew out a lungful of smoke and fanned the air, despite the breeze.

"Huh. I know Dad was religious, but I thought he'd gotten a grip—no offense—just 'Lamb of God' was the name of a metal band I used to . . . Anyway, I'm sure you guys came up with the name first."

"You're George's daughter." He grinned, unfurling into a rangy man with the stooped posture of a boy who got too tall too fast. His eyes were an arresting combination of amber and hazel. She accepted his extended hand for a shake. Not only was the grip firm, but his touch also precipitated a brief twitching in her uterus. But this might've been aftershocks of brazen public sex.

"I'm Gina. I have poor self-editing skills."

"Joshua."

"Why do you seem familiar?"

"You went to school with my little brother, Rick. Nielsen. Played baseball?"

"Woah. Nosepick Rick?"

"Yup. Nickname stuck through junior high."

"Is he here, too? Are you both, um, church members?"

"He died years ago. Near Kandahar."

Gina's heart dead-dropped into her stomach.

"But he's always with me." Mr. Beige tapped his chest with the cigarette hand, sending embers off with the wind.

"Shi-oot. I'm so sorry for your loss. God. So awful." Unable to withstand the emo onslaught, Gina clapped both hands over her eyes, freeing the weeping, unhinged idiot within. Poor little nose-picking bastard. Dead. Dead as Dad. Dead as her career. *Dead, dead, dead.*

"Do you need some water? Or Kleenex?"

"I'll be okay in a sec."

Mr. Beige stubbed the ciggie on his boot. "I quit smoking for two years, then started up again last month. I intend to quit again before Independence Day."

She sniffed, inhaling dramatically. "I quit drinking *and* drugs four years ago, but started drinking again last year, then quit again. Now I'm addicted to coffee." She stanched the tears on her sleeve. "Please remind me of your name."

"Joshua."

"Joshua Nielsen. I'm terrible with names, Joshua. Even saying your name, Joshua, again, it'll go *pfft* the minute you walk away."

He nodded at her duffel. "Take that for you?"

"I can handle it."

"But you don't have to."

"I'm okay."

"You plan on staying here, in the house?"

"Yes, why? Is that a problem? Is it haunted? It is, right?"

"I wouldn't know. Old, though." He headed for the door. "There are some nice motels hereabouts."

"I can't afford a motel."

Mr. Beige opened the screen, whispered back: "Folks are offering their tributes."

This was not in the plan. All she wanted was to shower off Yannick-residue and sleep.

"After you." He held the door in the manner men often do, standing on the threshold with an arm keeping it open, resulting in an awkward passing between crotch and door frame. His polite expression never changed while she bumped past with her luggage.

A last gulp of fresh air, then she entered a dim room pungent with carnations.

# Chapter Three

Dark. So dark. All the curtains shut. The only interior lights came from the parlor, which she couldn't see through the dozens of people in somber clothing gathered before the coffin.

Beyond the archway of the parlor, an old woman's voice droned in the tenor of someone finishing a story: "...he rented a carpet cleaner and came over to do all my rugs, even the den! And he wouldn't take a nickel for his efforts."

Voices murmured with approval of George's altruism. When her vision acclimated, Gina spied a pile of white hair, presumably from the speaker, who stood next to the coffin's open lid.

*Open lid.*

"He was always so helpful after my Oly died. Now they're together in heaven playing backgammon."

Gina shrugged off her duffel, and it landed on the wood floor with a thud. The crowd about-faced to stare at the outsider.

"Hey, everybody." Gina instantly regretted her ironically chipper voice. Instead of smiles or frowns, the mourners offered her variations of nods, from a full chin up-chin down to an almost imperceptible tilt. In return, Gina spun a half-circle, waving like British royalty.

Then came a rustling and hubbub before the crowd parted, opening a pathway from the coffin to Gina, into which a figure blazed a trail to her. Backlit by parlor lights, an auburn Elvis pompadour was the first distinguishing feature, followed by a face oozing with theatrical pity.

"Gina Fade, the prodigal daughter," said the man. "Prodigal daughter comes home. Such a shame to lose a daddy. Everyone, here is George's daughter."

Gina wished she could transmogrify into a shadow and slink away, but it was too late. Here was a VIP of some sort. Perfumed with cheap musk, his intense green eyes heat-missiled into hers with the fire of Rasputin, and he had the kind of fish lips she imagined were often wrapped around all-you-can-eat shrimp.

"I guess you didn't get my message about the viewing, Gina. I'm Pastor Thornton—Ed, Pastor Ed—of the Lamb of God Assembly." He stuck out his hand. She had no choice but to shake it. Clammy. Soft. Big surprise.

"Yeah, no, I didn't get any messages. Do you even have my number?"

"Come see how wonderful George looks in his eternal slumber." Doughy fingers wrapped around her wrist.

*Holy shit, no, no,* Gina's mind rapid-fired as he steered her through the gathering. Faces swiveled with murmured condolences. Her cheeks burned. How did she look compared to all these people dressed in Sunday church clothes? She, in her hoodie, yoga pants, and flip-flops, reeked of a coastal elite browsing for cheese at Trader Joe's, and probably of recent sex.

Up at ground zero, large vases stuffed with carnations

stood by the shiny metal coffin resting on a bier. Acknowledging this seminal moment, Gina steeled herself as she approached. She'd never seen a metal coffin before, or a dead body up close. Mom's dad and Dad's parents had died before she was born. At Grandma's funeral, she'd cowered in a pew with her eyes on her lap. And of all the drunks and junkies in her life who'd died, only Jasper had a funeral, but it was a closed-casket since he'd shot himself.

Pastor Ed let her go when they reached the coffin, but stayed close.

Dad's skin was a light shade of waxen yellow. Her artist's eye assessed the bronze dusting under his brows, the dyed black hair coiffed into a weird curl arranged on his forehead, the freshly shaved chin.

Outside, wind squalls blended eerily with the quiet susurrations of people studying her from the shadows of the living room. Her eyes left Dad to examine the space. The parlor was always his realm. She hadn't remembered his vast collection of VHS tapes, DVDs, Jesus bookends, or the TV Guides filling four long shelves in the built-in bookcase.

Someone cleared their throat behind her. Another coughed. Gina turned around. Did the Lambs of God expect words from her?

Nope. They wanted Pastor Ed to speak. Soon he was slinging his well-perfumed beef around, working the crowd.

"The Lord will wipe away every tear from our eyes, and death shall be no more, neither by mourning, nor crying, nor pain anymore..."

Everyone rubbernecked between her, the pastor, and Dad's remains.

"The tears, the anguish, the struggles, they will have all passed away, my friends. These will have all passed away."

Gina noticed Mr. Beige standing alongside a trio of

even beiger men. Older, chubbier, indistinguishable from each other, they had their reverent faces pinned to their pastor. "Here he lies. Never again to tread the earth or enjoy a carnival. He is at peace. For there is only peace now for George."

Oh. Tragic. Nothing left for him. A mob of church folk and the estranged daughter had invaded his house. Was Dad somehow aware of this? Did he and Oly pause their backgammon game to listen? If she hadn't waited so long to make plans to visit him, he might have taught her to play.

"Shit."

Gina clamped a hand over her mouth. Her outburst triggered a thorny silence. Then a second helping of tears for the day. These were the same tears she got watching animal rescue videos before the happy ending, or when a client scolded her. Helpless tears. Sad tears. Tears of regret at not visiting Dad the first time she'd gotten sober. She'd be a backgammon expert by now, goddamnit.

She forced herself to stop, raking her sleeve across her wet face. What a flippant, tacky, open-wound-of-a-woman they must think her. "Sorry, everyone." Nobody responded. Too busy gawking at something behind her.

Up high on the parlor's wall, a small oval window alternated between pearly gray light and blackness.

"Storm's on its way," said Pastor Ed.

# Chapter Four

The pastor's proclamation had the effect of a starter pistol, prompting a stampede in wooshes of wool blends as the mourners gathered coats and children.

An old lady stopped to hug Gina. "My sincerest condolences."

"Thank you." Gina drank in the scent of warm tater tots and rose-scented powder.

"I used to teach you in first grade." Gina first recognized the voice as the lady who'd been cooing about how helpful Dad was with the carpet cleaning, but now she flashed on a younger version of the face, with big, round eyes and pin curls.

"Mrs. Olson?"

"Bingo." She beamed, showing off dimples before handing Gina her coat. "Little help?"

"Oh, sure." Gina dutifully guided a sleeve over Mrs. Olson's outstretched arm.

"You were always my special helper, weren't you?"

"I wish I had a better memory."

"You passed out papers for me. Remember that?"

"I think so. Other arm."

Mrs. Olson moved her purse and extended the other arm. "Do you remember when you passed out the cupcakes for Valentine's Day? And you, you sneaky girl, you licked the frosting on top before handing them to the other kids?"

"Wow. I do, actually. Except I only licked a single cupcake and gave it to a boy I had a crush on who's dead now."

"What's that?"

Behind Mrs. Olson, Mr. Beige nodded goodbye and left.

Gina fluffed up Mrs. Olson's collar. "All done."

"You were such an odd little girl, oh my." She patted Gina's cheek.

"Circumstances weren't optimal, but it was nice seeing you today, Mrs. Olson."

"Yes, dear. So nice. I'll need a bit of wind at my back to keep ahead of the storm." She squeezed Gina's arm. "We left you food in the fridge."

"Oh, thank you."

"Will you be at the funeral?"

"I kind of have to be."

"That's right. Well, here I go." She tossed Gina a kiss. Holy shit, that's what she did every Friday. She'd say, "Have a blessed weekend, children," and then blow everyone a kiss.

Mrs. Olson waddled outside behind Pastor Ed's puffy-haired wife and three toddlers.

The pastor hung back with the air of a captain overseeing passengers abandoning his ship. Once the place emptied, he jangled a set of keys in a way suggesting she was being summoned. But Gina didn't budge. Finally, he strolled over to her with a snide smirk pasted on his florid face.

"The funeral folks will be here by nine sharp tomorrow to take him to Lamb of God and on over to Wilson Cemetery afterwards," he said. "Fifteen miles northwest of Ellsworth, not far."

"Wait, what? He's going to stay here?"

"Until tomorrow."

"Is that even legal?"

"Certainly."

"If you say so."

"Here." He handed her a keychain, heavy from the weight of a dozen keys plus a bottle opener. "The big key is for the front door. There's the barn . . . his truck, which is not in the best condition. The other keys are mysteries. I doubt you need the bottle opener."

"Why do you doubt that?"

"Not my place." He held up his hands. Gina frowned at his fancy pinky ring with a gleaming diamond in the center of the onyx, enhancing his "1970s country superstar" affectations.

"I know this must be hard for you, Gina. You did good with all this, with all the folks who came today. Your Daddy must be looking down on you and smiling."

"Thanks." She resented the warm fuzzies his compliment gave her.

"The funeral begins at ten sharp tomorrow at Lamb of God. Up in Ellsworth." He doffed an invisible hat to her and then to George III. "See you both then."

The screen door banged shut behind him as he went out to join the wife and kids waiting by the champagne Cadillac parked close to the house. The wind sent everyone's hair flying except his.

"Why can't they come get him tonight?" Gina yelled through the screen.

"Closing time was five sharp."

Dirt billowed as the caddy drove off. Icy air blew through the screen. Whiskey weather. *Damn.* At the first thunderclap, she closed the door. Alone with Dad now.

# Alone with Dad

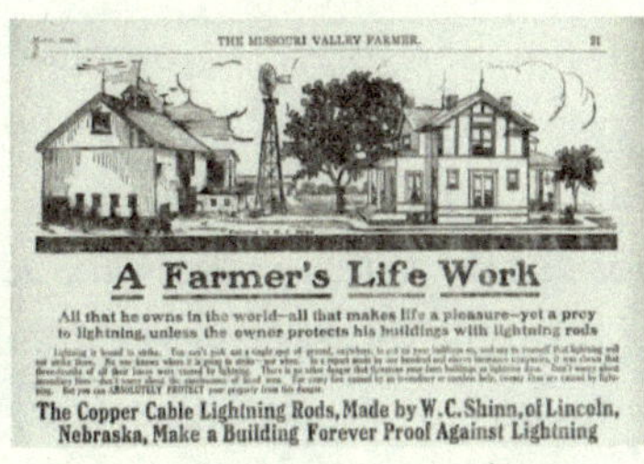

# Chapter Five

Gina rested her forehead on the door. Unusual energy buzzed around her. Of her own making, yes, and abetted by a creepy house filled with disjointed memories and a storm taking shape outside.

She peeked through the lace side-curtain at a horizon clotted with branches of lightning spiking to earth like upside-down fireworks. The sight of the rental car consoled her, though. Escape, if necessary, sat parked a mere twenty feet off the porch.

When she couldn't find a reason to keep herself pointed at the front door and windows, she turned. From the dark of the living room, the parlor shone bright beyond its archway. An overhead pendant light beamed down on the coffin, giving her the unsettling sensation of being the solo audience member waiting for a show to begin. She imagined a disembodied voice announcing, "Ladies and gentlemen, the remains of Mr. Fade will soon impress you with its feats of prestidigitation!"

God, it was quiet here.

Tomorrow, she'd tackle the myriad of tasks ahead of her.

Tonight, she'd get some sleep. She half-heartedly nudged the duffel bag with her foot, but, in classic Gina style, she rejected the pragmatic course of action and took a step closer to the coffin.

Was Dad drunk when he died? He'd sworn up and down he'd stopped drinking soon after she and Mom left. But during a phone call six months ago, he'd slurred his half of the conversation, admitted to falling off the wagon, and ranted about his own drunk father and the inevitability of Gina's alcoholism. He also told her the church let him down, but didn't elaborate. Then, not two weeks later, a sober George recounted all the fun he had at the church carnival.

Hard to imagine the group she'd seen today whooping it up on the Tilt-A-Whirl. Hypothetical images of grim-faced evangelicals praising Jesus on the swing carousel or shooting water guns at balloons all boiled down to a single image: Mr. Beige as a film noir Johnny, all chisel-faced with a ciggie hanging out the side of his mouth and eyes squinted at a table full of old soda bottles. He tosses a ring, and it lands perfectly! Then gifts Gina with the prize, which is his big, stiff, stuffed—

*Tick, tick, tick.*

In her reverie, Gina had taken a dozen steps in Dad's direction when the ticking sound drew her over to the fireplace, a humble brick design with a blackened hearth and antique brass fire screen. On its mantel, sandwiched between a painting of Jesus and a framed photo Gina's kindergarten picture, stood an old domed clock with Bavarian details and fancy gold numbers. She wondered if it might fetch two hundred dollars. Or more?

*Tick, tick, tick.*

The room full of people must have absorbed its sound

earlier. Or maybe it seemed louder now that she'd noticed it. Filigree clock hands clicked to six p.m., followed by the chime preamble: *Dee-dah-dee-dah, dee-dah-dee-dah.* Six ensuing chimes clanged with the intensity of church bells.

*DING.* This sound! She was grateful for a memory neither good nor bad. The clock just was. Always was.

*DING.* Inside his gold frame, handsome white Jesus with lustrous hair and hipster beard gazed up at his heavenly daddy.

*DING.* Six-year-old Gina's smile showed off a missing front tooth. Her frame was the same as Jesus' frame.

*DING.* Gina rotated in a circle, remembering the massive, ancient television with a small flat-panel on top of it. She'd always watched TV on the flat-panel and couldn't recall the big TV being anything more than a piece of furniture.

*DING.* The green velvet couch, still covered in Mom's hand-knit throws, was, by the looks of things, still in great condition. Cha-ching!

*DING.* Seeing the dark stairwell, she realized she wasn't ready to go upstairs.

As the chime's resonance faded, the *tick, tick, ticks* resumed.

Gina figured if she had to share the house until tomorrow morning at nine a.m. *sharp*, she should come to peace with the idea of Dad's body being here all night. So, she headed into the parlor to shut the coffin lid.

Dozens of halting baby steps later, she sidled up alongside the coffin and knocked on its side.

"Dad?" she began in a whisper. Then, "Dad?" Louder, now, not because she was nuts enough to think he'd respond, but because he *didn't* answer her, which made talking to a corpse less dicey.

A new feeling gripped her: the indifference of mortality. This was no longer her dad. It was the cadaver of a man who, according to Mom, had gone so loco for Jesus, he'd lost his family and his mind.

Gina leaned closer, breathing through her mouth in case his decay was stronger than the carnations. She noted the area where the electrical current exited his body. A discolored flap of skin hung off his left cheek near his ear. The pancake makeup putty they'd spackled on top had collapsed, allowing yellowish leakage to drain onto the satin pillow.

His final mortal word had been "Gina," followed by his last scream, sighs, and a giggle. She thought he'd been joking, though he wasn't the type to do that. Worse, she'd stayed on the line waiting for his punchline but heard nothing more than a strange electrical buzz. She finally hung up and dialed 911, then endured another agonizing six minutes as the dispatcher tried to reach someone in Ellsworth County.

The pillow stain bugged her to distraction. She reached down to his jacket shoulder, wincing when her fingers made contact, then tugged it until it covered the stain. Now the sleeve rode up his wrist, revealing the small leather book under his hands. Who'd placed this here? Who'd seen it? None of the guests, obviously. Gina carefully dislodged it, taking care to avoid contact with his flesh, and silently willed the fingers not to break off or some such nightmare shit.

"Why was this going with you, Pops?"

## Chapter Six

Written inside the cover in faded ink, it said *George Fade, 1924.*

Either somebody understood its significance to him, or it contained information they wanted to keep secret. Was the original George Fade a gangster with a client list? Were these confessions? Blackmail notes? Hypotheticals banged into each other like bumper cars. Gina fanned its pages, imagining a gold doubloon or a winning lottery ticket, but finding only page after page of neatly printed words from George Fade the First. It was a diary. Of course.

She fanned it open. "Hello, Great . . . Great-Granddad." Pages accordioned, then stopped.

*June 12, 1924.* Same date as today, more than a century ago.

She needed a sweater but didn't want to go upstairs. Instead, she curled up on Dad's corduroy recliner, creeped out at first, then sank into its warmth as she settled in to read the entry.

*Today was what Father called a scorcher. It got to ninety*

*degrees by noon. Then it rained in the late afternoon. I have been enjoying the break from school, even with the additional chores. Summers sure go by quickly. I continue to read Arthur Conan Doyle's Round the Fire Stories. A particular favorite line is, "I writhed, I struggled, I broke through the bonds of sleep, and I burst with a shriek into my own life."*

*Mother made fried chicken and mulberry pie. The sun did not set until after eight o'clock. I was able to finish my kite before it got dark. Tom's kite is larger, although heavy. He may have a hard time catching the wind.*

*Before bedtime I read Philippians chapter two, in which Paul asks for unity and tells us to be of the same mind. We should not fight.*

Subsequent pages contained the same boring tally of summer days filled with farm work, kite flying, warm temperatures, and afternoon storms. Gina speculated on how much this glimpse into the past might net. Her brain had become a veritable spreadsheet of items and their approximate worth.

On the next page, a newspaper clipping with Scotch Tape at its corners told of the death by lightning strike of a boy named Tom Cooper on June 23, 1924.

Oh no! Heavy-kite Tom?

Below the clipping, young George had written:

*Everyone from school attended Tom's funeral. His parents did not join anyone in saying 'amen.' Nor did they appear comforted by condolences or prayers. Nobody was invited to their house afterwards.*

*Mother said I should never have mixed with those people.*

*The casket stayed closed. Everyone whispered about the condition of the body. Only the mortician, I and his parents knew for certain how he looked. I was unhappy to be amongst this group. I do not want to remember Tom at the end.*

*His father took me aside and asked me to recount the death. I told him I didn't see the lightning strike his son. I hope God will forgive my lie.*

*I will never tell a soul what I saw. Not even Mom.*

"Ooh. What *did* you see, Great-Great-Gramps?"

On the next page, an article from the Ellsworth Reporter dated two weeks later, on July 7, 1924, recounted another lightning accident, or near-accident. George Fade, age fourteen, survived a strike by ground lightning. *"He suffers from ringing in the ears but is otherwise healthy."* In the sepia photograph, a frowning boy who looked like her dad posed for the picture in front of his house—*this* house—in which she currently stood by the coffin of his now-deceased great-grandson, George Fade III. The circle of life.

Dad never mentioned specific relatives, only that the Fades suffered similar afflictions. Reconnecting after all these years had her so keyed up and preoccupied by the demands of sobriety, perhaps she heard wrong. Was everyone nuts? No. It was the drink. A family of drunks. The Fades anesthetized themselves due to a lack of coping skills.

After the article came a chunk of torn-out pages followed by blank pages. The only time she tore pages from *her* diaries was to ensure no prying eyes. What did George want to hide?

A last look at Dad, then she reached for the lid but paused before dropping it.

Several things bothered her. On their video calls, Dad wore denim—a denim vest, or jacket, or shirt, or coveralls—because he loved the denim. Instead, they'd dressed him in a cheap suit. If she had more energy, she'd consider digging through his closet for that 80s bomber jacket he sometimes wore on their calls. But the thought of hoisting his carcass into a sitting position and forcing stiff arms into jacket sleeves torpedoed the idea.

Also, why bury him at all? Why not cremation? Mr. Beige mentioned "George's wishes." She had to find the will. Or ask the pastor. He seemed privy to it all, except for the denim.

There was also the weird black curl on Dad's forehead, giving him a magician vibe. In their video calls he always wore his hair slicked back, so why the spit curl?

She steeled herself, reached for the curl. Did more electricity bust out through his skull, and the mortician made a curl to cover the exit wound? Hardened with hair product, it wouldn't be brushed aside. So, she got a finger underneath and flipped it up.

"Holy shit!"

Someone had drawn a black cross on his forehead.

# Chapter Seven

On closer inspection, the cross was made of ash. She swiped at it with her index finger, cringing at the cold skin, then gasped at the sight of the bisected cross, which exposed the grayish flesh beneath. She felt ghoulish wiping her finger on the coffin's satin lining. Who the hell touches a corpse this way? Jesus!

"Sorry. I'm sorry I did that. Uh. So long, Pop. I never called you Pop to your face. Not officially. So, if we ever sat together on the front porch drinking soda, I'd say, 'I'm having a pop with Pop.'"

She reached for the head panel but stopped upon noticing a ratty yellow handkerchief peeking out of Dad's jacket pocket. The edges disintegrated when she attempted to fluff it up. Fragments stuck to her fingers. She blew them off, then inched the item from his pocket. Here was another old newspaper clipping from the Ellsworth Reporter, dated 1953. Why wasn't this in the diary?

Its headline read: "George Fade on Trial for Multiple Murders." The court drawing depicted a middle-aged George the First on the witness stand. Although sketched in profile, the artist had caught his prominent scowl. He seemed to be mad-dogging the jury, or a witness, or the prosecutor.

What the hell? Murder? A murderer in the family? That never came up in conversation. Not once.

His resemblance to her dad was uncanny. He had the same dark, stringy hair, square jaw, and high cheekbones, plus the long, slender nose and slight overbite. Same as hers. Why bury this with George the Third? Disguising it as a handkerchief? And why hadn't she heard about this dude? She wanted to call Mom, except the last she looked, her phone had 19% battery left and the charger was buried at the bottom of her duffel.

Sudden fatigue overwhelmed her. If not careful, she'd slump over the coffin and wind up asleep with her head on Dad's chest. She yawned, placed the newspaper clipping into the diary to keep for posterity, and tucked the diary into her waistband. Shame filled her. The way she'd studied him, removing items from his person with the precision of a grave robber.

She switched off the parlor lights at the same time chain lightning burst outside the little oval window. It lit up the parlor in three pulses, splashing a light show across George's wax-dummy face. Disconcerted, she turned the lights back on, but chickened out on closing the coffin, opting instead to escape into the living room, where the familiar *tick, tick, tick* of the clock greeted her.

Under the ticking, the winds swept through the trees, battering the house, announcing the storm to come. Wood beams whined in duress, and she'd swear the floor swelled back and forth like an old wooden ship. The rhythm of it aligned with the tick-tick-tick. Any more of this and she'd slip into a hypnotic state.

Somewhere close behind her came a whine, as if someone had stepped on a bad floorboard.

"Fuck!" Adrenaline bugged out her eyes, constricted her muscles. She wheeled around to the sound. Nobody stood there. Of course not. She was alone.

Or not. Another creak to her side. She raised her arms as a shield, cringing and unable to look for fear of what she might see.

"Stop it, goddamn you, stop it!"

She darted over to the nearest lamp and clicked it on. A hundred watts blinded her before the bulb crapped out.

*Tick, tick, tick . . .*

"Is someone still here?"

*Tick, tick, tick . . .*

She eyed her duffel, calculating how long it would take to grab it and run out to the rental car, find a motel—but no, no, no. She needed to stay on task. Close the house. Find stuff to sell. Locate and talk to the lawyer. Get the money. Then goodbye.

Gina pressed her weight onto the floorboards until they produced a groan. Relief swelled. She'd made the sound. A good enough explanation to hang on to for now.

Except . . .

The sudden puff of air on her neck.

She coiled into a spring, fists clenched, ready to whirl around in a bombardment of punches and kicks.

"If someone is inside this house and doesn't get the fuck out, I'm calling the police!"

She waited a tense few seconds, imagining a roommate who wouldn't reveal himself and hid in the walls. Shit. Too many horror films in rehab. Time for saner rationalizations. Okay. The house was old, ergo, the wind squeezed through its spaces and tickled her neck. *Yes.* The explanation eased her journey around the downstairs portion of the house to shut off the lights.

When all except the parlor lights were out and when she couldn't avoid it anymore, she got her bag and stood at the base of the stairs staring up at its chasm of blackness.

"Here I come. Mess with me and I'll jump your ass like a psychotic chimpanzee. I'll dig into your eye sockets. I will fucking bite!"

## Chapter Eight

Every squeak of wood underfoot set off a mini horror show reeling through her head. She imagined a stair collapsing and her foot falling through and getting torn up by the wood shards and a nail slicing open her calf, which would then give her tetanus, which she knew fuck about. Lockjaw? Something terrible.

At the top step, she paused and turned, confirming Dad's body hadn't somehow escaped eternal confinement to crawl up to its own bed. She flipped on the light up top. An old yellow bulb illuminated a landing still carpeted with the orange shag she used to pretend was hot lava. Four closed doors surrounded her.

The first door led into the bathroom. She'd have to visit it soon, so she turned on the light, made sure the toilet was clean, and nothing lurked behind Dad's mildewy Roy Rogers shower curtain.

Door number two opened into what used to be her room but now functioned as junk storage. Boxes filled every space, along with several vacuum cleaners and old bikes. No pictures on the walls. Still the same tiny single bed, neatly made with nothing on it. She'd expected to sleep in here tonight, but had grown far too tall for the bed.

She remembered the mint green curtains. Mom made them for her, modeled after Cinderella's bedroom curtains. She added hand-stitched ivy and rosebuds twining around butterflies. These curtains inspired Gina to pursue a career in design. Now she nosed between them to look out at the barn, filled with a sense of bad memories but nothing specific. A place Dad disappeared into. A place he forbade her to enter without permission.

A kid's Bible story collection stood between two wooden dove statues functioning as bookends. They sat atop a desk. Dad had replaced her princess desk with a mammoth mid-century tanker, a gray metal utilitarian beauty with three drawers on the left, two on the right, and a shallow center drawer. With a minimum of cleanup effort, she'd easily get four grand from some rich hipster looking to spruce up their mid-century home office.

On to the master bedroom. She cracked the door a few inches, snaking her hand around the frame to switch on the light. Inside, an unmade king-sized bed, plus the scent of cologne and dirty clothes. She stepped into the room, unable to relinquish the idea of being an intruder in the museum of an unintentionally abandoned life. A few days ago, Dad probably walked from the bathroom to his bedroom. He took a dump and a shower. He slapped his cheeks with cologne. Now, here *she* was, a shadow skulking around in his tomb.

Cripes, there were a lot of Jesus pictures on his walls. Jesus with lambs, Jesus with children, Jesus on a motorcycle and not wearing a helmet. Idiot. She left the light on but closed the door.

Bedroom number three, formerly the guest room,

contained a dresser and a nightstand next to a queen bed, and the inoffensive scent pairing of dust and old wood. She dropped the duffel next to the dresser, dug out her charger, and plugged her phone into an outlet. The journal went on the nightstand.

She yanked off the bedspread, braced for critters then relaxed when nothing scuttled across the clean linens. Next, an inspection of the mattress edges for bedbugs. Finding none, she did a final check by banging both hands on the mattress, mushrooming up a dust cloud and a coughing fit.

As a former Girl Scout and rehab veteran with a dose of germ phobia, Gina had come prepared. From her duffel, she pulled out a flat sheet to drape over the bedspread and pillow, and a thick wool coat Mom gave her. Gina had little need for it in Southern California. Now she'd use it as a blanket.

She noted the Jesus-on-the-cross painting on the wall above the bed. Mother Mary and Mary Magdalene wept at his feet. Was Dad a Catholic? Or was this a Mom remnant? Next to this picture hung a downright adorable, framed child's watercolor of Mom and Dad and little pig-tailed Gina on the porch. Some of her earliest work. She painted the house well, perspective-wise. She'd given Dad bright blue eyes instead of his browns. There were two more renditions of Dad—one in an upstairs window and a young-boy version of Dad in the living room window. All Dad iterations had those crazy baby blues.

The picture troubled her but she couldn't pinpoint the reason. She felt like someone in a horror movie whose kid draws a dark vortex in class instead of a flower, and everyone goes, "Uh oh."

Unrelenting wind rattled the windows. Night after

night of this could easily have driven her batshit crazy if she were a nineteenth-century homesteader pulled away from a New England village to live in a flat, inhospitable place.

She smacked the window frame until it loosened enough to shut it.

Time to sleep. Her body and brain demanded it. Lying down would come in stages. First, she sat, bouncing a little to test the give of the mattress. Stage two: lie back onto the pillow. Okay. To think, twenty-four hours ago, she was on a plane. Twenty-four hours before that, she was in an AA meeting bitching about getting on a plane.

A buzzing sound interrupted her thoughts.

# Chapter Nine

Was it coming from the closet? She stared at the closet door, willing the noise to stop.

*Bzz-bzz-bzz.*

No. It was behind her, on the other side of the wall.

Oh shit. Maybe it was coming from *inside* the wall. But why would somebody hide in the wall? What was the name of that New Zealand horror movie? Some freaky dude named Eugene lived in the wall. Good movie.

*Bzz-bzz-bzz.*

She pressed her ear against the wall. If someone's voice whispered a hello, she'd piss herself. Definitely.

It made no sense, though. If somebody were hiding in the wall, would they even want to say hello? Must be they're hiding for a reason. So why announce themselves?

*They're waiting for me to sleep.*

"Stop!" she growled to herself. The noise stopped. Gina froze, eyes wide.

The winds beat the house with a ferocity that got her worrying about trees uprooting. Same fear she had in LA when the warm Santa Ana winds blew down from the mountains, stripping palm trees of their fronds and oak trees of their weaker branches.

*Bzz-bzz-bzz.*

Okay, the noise was definitely coming from the room behind the wall: the master bedroom. Was it Dad phoning her from the great beyond? *Great.* She wrapped the coat around her and got out of bed.

*Bzz-bzz-bzz.*

In the hallway now, locked in a stare-down with her dad's closed door. Closer, she caught whiffs of his laundry and cologne. It felt as though he'd be coming back any minute. How does someone just die and leave behind their still-alive smells?

*Bzz-bzz-bzz.*

On the count of three, she whipped the door open, adrenaline readying to punch a ghost or a stowaway guest.

*Bzz-bzz-bzz.*

Through the piles of shoes and dirty laundry, she zeroed in on a mound of clothing draped over a chair. She pulled clothes off what turned out to be a blue velvet club chair and found the cell phone Dad rarely used. Several times, he'd called from his landline to ask her to dial his cell so the ring would tell him where he'd left it.

The caller ID said, "Unknown."

She answered. "Hello? Uh, George's phone."

"Georgie, is that you?" The voice, rasping, tremulous, could have been male or female.

"No, this is his daughter."

In response, the rattle of labored breathing.

"Are you still there?"

"Is he dead?"

"Yes, I'm afraid so—"

"Lord, Lord God!"

"May I ask—?"
"Don't let it see you!"
"What?
"Do not let it see you, girl!"
"Who?"
Dial tone.

# Chapter Ten

This absurd warning from some spooky person who knew her Dad was just the thing she needed for a good night's sleep. *Do not let it see you, girl!*

She considered calling them back, but tonight wasn't the night to freak herself out even more than she already had. She turned down the ringer and brought Dad's cell back with her, placing it on the nightstand near the diary.

"Keep me safe, Momma," she said, as if Mom could hear her a thousand miles west.

She wrapped herself in the coat, reached to switch off the light, but stopped when she saw the diary. Ugh. The light would stay on, she decided as she rolled to her side, facing the window. Occasional blips of light pulsed behind its thin white curtains.

Instead of sleep, her mind played an extended medley of mistakes, worries, and recriminations while the winds kept a steady beat on the house. If she had bourbon, just one little shot, it would melt her down into a buttery puddle of unimpeded slumber. Now her reliance on alcohol, even as a fond recollection, made it into the litany of issues keeping her jittery and awake.

A jarring timpani of thunder announced a new storm. Or was this a continuation of the previous storm? Torrential rain followed. Could old George's house withstand it?

At some point, the rain became too hard to ignore. There must be leaks. Did she hear a drip-drip-drip?

*No. Yes. No. Yes. Shit.*

Sighing, she sat up and slipped into her flip-flops. The buzzing, the phone call, and her unhinged imagination had toughened her up enough that she went through the motions of checking each room upstairs without bugging out. No drips found. It was tempting to fall back into bed, but no. Wood damage would reduce the home value. She had to go downstairs and check.

Somehow, she made it down the stairwell and through a dark living room, past a bright parlor with an open coffin, and into the kitchen. Here she found both a leak by the back door and a big empty pot on top of the stove. Too easy? Too bad. Another win was opening the fridge and confirming the Lambs of God had left four different slabs of casserole in separate glass containers, as Mrs. Olson had mentioned. A plate of cheesy carbs triggered salivation, except she didn't have the energy to look for silverware.

She needed to close the coffin. Two steps into the parlor and the lights blinked out. She bemoaned her lack of a phone or the foresight to have searched for a flashlight or candles while in the kitchen.

Thunder boom-boom-boomed like a million fists from hell pounding on a thin door.

Lightning bathed the parlor in false daylight.

Something moved!

The lightning snapped off.

Thunder in the darkness.

Another pulse brightened the room.

And she saw what had moved.

Dad's head rose from its satin pillow. His face had frozen into the stiff, neutral expression of a ventriloquist's dummy.

"No! No!"

The pulse ended, leaving behind darkness even darker than before.

At the next pulse, the eyes opened. His gleaming blues pierced into her browns.

Gina's knees turned to jelly.

Another burst, and Dad's lips parted. The mortician's stitches tore through his dead flesh, squirting embalming fluid on his chin as the lips formed into a giant O.

She had no words. No grunts. No cries. No heartbeat. No thoughts.

A lightning bolt shot out of his frayed mouth and shattered the parlor window. Wind and rain blew in sideways through the broken glass.

Gina's vision blurred as she roused, turning around, getting the fuck out. The continuous lightning strikes surrounding the house gave the effect of her running in slow-motion.

"Oh, shit, shit, shit!" She stumbled her way up the staircase, expecting that a dead man's hands would burst through the carpet to grab at her ankles and pull her back downstairs.

## Chapter Eleven

Gina banged into the bedroom, pulled her cell phone from the charger. Only 7% left. "Damn!" She pushed a button on the phone, then dove under her coat. It took three rings before a woman's "Hello?"

"Momma!"

"Who is this?"

"Something really bad happened!"

"Gina?"

Gina struggled to slow her breathing. "Yes, it's Gina! Sorry."

"Gina Ballerina."

"He was staring at me!"

"Who was?"

"Dad. He's a monster!"

"Shhh . . . Listen to my voice. You listening?"

"Yeah."

"Are you in danger?"

"Hold on." Gina lowered the phone, ears straining for

whatever sound a reanimated corpse might make. "I don't know."

"Is someone there with you?"

"No. Yes. Does Dad count?"

"Where are you?"

"Upstairs." Gina's voice had segued from near-hyperventilation to a babyish whine.

"Good, my little Gina Ballerina."

"His body is *downstairs*."

"Who?"

"Dad!" She winced at her volume. "Sorry."

"Why is Dad downstairs?"

"The church people left him here until tomorrow." Violent shivering wracked her shoulders and arms, making it difficult to hold the phone.

"Gina Ballerina had a bad dream."

"No. A lightning bolt shot out of his mouth!"

"It's not real. Go downstairs to check. Take me with you."

"Momma, no, I can't go down there."

"You can."

Why was it so easy for others—and herself, for that matter—to attribute what she saw to a bad dream or a hallucination? Nobody ever believes alcoholics and drug addicts. Shit, she didn't believe herself.

"Gina Ballerina faces her fears these days, yes?" Week after week, Mom's voice grew ever more sing-songy. Pretty soon, she'd sound like Glinda the Good Witch or a cartoon daisy.

"Yeah. I'll go check." Gina draped the coat over her shoulders and headed to the door. "PS, all the fucking lights are out thanks to the storm."

"Do you need to use the bad words all the time?"

"Yes, I damn well do."

Mom chuckled, doing worlds of good for Gina to hear.

"Okay, I'm on the stairs. This place is so creepy. How did you stand it?"

"When I lived there, it was very nice."

"Shit, it's almost eleven. The clock is gonna chime in a minute."

Mom hummed the noises of the clock.

Parlor lights clicked on, startling Gina.

"Okay, we have light!"

"Go to your Dad. You'll see it was only a bad dream."

"Okay." Gina approached the coffin, resting a hand on her chest in case she needed to punch her heart back to life. "He's inside." Waxen, eyes shut, mouth closed.

"Only a dream, yes?"

Gina lowered the coffin's heavy lid. "It felt a hundred percent real, Momma."

The mantel clock began its preamble.

"I'm going back upstairs."

*DING*. Silence on the other end. "Hello?" The phone was dead. "Shit!"

*DING*. She ran through the living room.

*DING*. And flew up the stairs.

*DING*. She crossed the landing to the guest room.

*Ding*. The chimes rang softer once Gina shut the door behind her.

*Ding*. She plugged in the phone and made sure it was charging this time.

*Ding*. All the ticking and creaking and rain and wind had conspired to give her an ass-kicking hallucinatory nightmare. The end.

*Ding*. Except that the diary was on the floor.

*Ding*. She must've bumped into the side table and knocked it off!

*Ding*. Bullshit. She crawled into bed. Something was toying with her. Maybe her own mind.

*Ding*. She curled into a fetal position and murmured every state in the country alphabetically.

---

Outside, between each violent coupling of air and fire, it watched her. With every bright lashing, curiosity and hunger mounted until there grew an overwhelming desire to know, *Who's in George's house? Who's in George's house? Who's in George's house?*

# Bye, Dad

LIGHTNING STRIKES FRED THIELEN HOME

Bolt Punctured Roof in Several Places, Filled House With Soot.

Lightning struck the residence of Fred Thielen west of the city this forenoon during the shower of rain. The bolt hit near the flue, made several holes in the roof, filled the house with soot and marred the interior. No fire followed the flash. Mrs. Thielen was in the house at the time but was not injured, however, she was much frightened. Mr. Thielen was working in a field nearby and saw the lightning strike his house.

# Chapter Twelve

Persistent knocking woke Gina from a dead sleep.

A male voice called out, "Good morning!"

Gina cowered under the coat, envisioning Dad's body dangling on marionette strings above the bed. "Miss Fade. We're here to pick up the deceased."

Oh! Flinging off the coat, she yelled at the light streaming through the curtains. "Hold on!" She wobbled over to unplug her phone from the wall, frowning at the 50% charge. Also, it was 7:43 a.m.

"Miss Fade? We're here to—"

"Hold on! Shit."

Gina banged on the window frame until it loosened, then raised it a few inches.

"You're early!"

A blond head peeked around the awning. "No, miss."

"Fine. Be right down!" On her way out, she noticed the diary back up on the nightstand again. "Fanfuckingtastic." She slipped into the coat and buttoned it as she plodded downstairs. It barely covered her ass.

The living room glowed in gauzy morning light. It could have been a snapshot of the past until she marched through, animating the dust on her way to the front door. She opened both the door and the screen, glaring at the figures in front of the low-hanging sun. "Hi."

Two guys in jeans and sweatshirts stood next to a casket trolley. Their heads hung half-bowed in respect for the mourner.

"Sorry for your loss, Miss Fade," said the older of the pair, a squatty blond dude with acne-scarred skin.

The other, a lanky Native kid in his late teens, nodded a sorry while eyeing her state of attire.

"Thanks. Why are you so early?"

"Pastor's order was to have the deceased set up at the Lamb of God Assembly by nine sharp," the blond said.

"Fine. Have at it." She stepped aside so they could enter.

The guys grunted and sped past her into the parlor. The casket had fallen off the bier, landing on its side with the lid open, expelling George's body the way a mouth spits out a piece of rancid meat. Gina cupped her own mouth, which did nothing to stifle her outcry. Dad's eyes were open, blank, dead, and staring at her.

"It's okay," the older man told her. "I've seen this before."

"You've seen *this* before? This is insane!" Gina fought for her breath.

"Nothing to worry about."

"No, it's not right, not right," she repeated, noting the shattered parlor window that was unbroken last night during her conversation with Mom.

"Everything is wet," the kid said under his breath.

"Lightning broke the window, which I thought was a dream." The men gave her blank faces. "I closed the lid and went to bed. I did nothing to cause this. Nothing."

On a count of three, they lifted George's remains back into his coffin. The kid coughed and gagged the entire time.

"Pastor Ed ain't gonna be happy about how he looks," the blond said, lowering the bier.

Gina, cringing between the front door and the parlor, wouldn't move a step closer.

"I came in from Burbank yesterday," she babbled as the duo wheeled the coffin through the living room. "When I got here, they were having a wake, which nobody told me about." She ran to hold the screen open for them. "I've never heard of leaving a body in a house overnight."

The pair lowered the trolley down the porch stairs.

"But seriously, is leaving the body in its home a thing out here?"

"Out where, ma'am?" the teen asked, drawing a frown from the older man.

"Never mind," said Gina.

They pushed Dad over to an old van painted hearse-black.

"I didn't mean to be insulting. Last night was a bitch. Sorry. Difficult times."

The men slid the coffin into the van and closed the doors.

Gina tried to stop herself, but couldn't. "Do you believe in ghosts?"

"Nah," said the kid. He and his boss got in the van.

"Okay. Cool. Thank you!" They thought she was crazy.

With the body gone from the house, everything improved. The makeshift hearse and its road dust didn't mar her view from the porch, so lovely and green, with a wide horizon beyond the trees and barn. Sunshine warmed her cheeks. A lovely morning. Clean air.

She dragged herself back to the parlor, exhausted from last night's and this morning's nightmares, glad it was over.

Turns out it wasn't over.

Within the coffin-shaped dry area on an otherwise damp Turkish rug sat a square of paper. Was this the clipping of the trial with the artist's rendering of George in the witness box? No. The trial clipping was upstairs.

"Balls!" She stomped over and picked it up. Oh. *Fun*! It *was* the newspaper article about the murder trial. When she first saw the sketch, George the First was in profile. Now the face looked squarely at the artist drawing him—or at the person looking at the picture. His eyes appeared fixed on her, and she knew that despite the black and white ink, they shone a bright blue.

Two different newspapers? No. The Ellsworth Reporter, same as the other. She ran hellbent upstairs, jiggled the diary, hoping to find a similar clipping, but nothing dropped loose. Flummoxed, she sat on the bed, unable to pull her gaze from the image.

*How did it get downstairs?*

In drunken days of yore, excuses unfurled into crazy choose-your-own-adventures but retained logical causation. "I drank a bottle of Jim Beam, then tried to steal pork rinds at 7-11 and woke up with a guy who spoke only French who gave me crabs." A+B+C = Crabs.

Either the drawing had changed, or she'd seen it wrong the first time. There were tons of instances in which she distrusted her perceptions, but as an artist, she *always* trusted her eyes. The figure had initially stood in profile.

A+B+C = The drawing itself changed.

"Don't let it see you," the unknown caller had warned her.

A breakdown would have to wait until after the funeral. She was already running late.

# Chapter Thirteen

On her drive to the church, Gina fantasized about what she'd say if forced to speak. "Hi, my name is Gina Fade, and I'm an alcoholic and drug addict, here to talk about a guy I barely knew, a guy Mom called 'the sperm donor.' Where's everyone from? How 'bout that pastor, eh? Hey, Pastor, the Dollar Store called. It wants its Elvis wig back."

As delightful as the ensuing discomfort might be, she'd be honest and admit there'd been a distance between herself and George in the last twenty-plus years. She'd temper it with a mention of their recent video calls, or a good memory from childhood, such as their one and only canoe trip when she and Dad wore hats and held fishing poles but didn't fish and were content only to glide along the muddy waters of the Smoky Hill River and train their binoculars on the riverbank where fat prairie chickens congregated. Some had bright orange sacs on their necks. Later that night and for weeks to come, she ran through her entire set of crayons, drawing pictures of those chickens. Similar colors now flew by as she drove. Burnt Sienna . . . Raw Sienna . . . Tumbleweed . . . Goldenrod . . . Atomic Tangerine.

Rural sparseness gave way to a small suburb. She noticed the top of the church before she got anywhere near it. The gold cross up top sparkled in the morning light.

Soon she was cruising across a vast and recently paved parking lot, with a mini mega-church in the middle, a white mushroom sprung up from the tar. She estimated about fifty vehicles already parked and glanced at the car clock. 9:59 a.m. The Lambs were punctual.

On her way inside, she read the church marquee.

<u>LAMB OF GOD CONGREGATION</u>
Sunday service 10 am & Bible Study after
Wednesday service 6 pm
Thursday Adult Bible Study 6 pm. Bingo 7:30
*Blessed are those who mourn, for they will be comforted.*
*Matthew 5:4*

SHE ALMOST STEPPED ON A PIECE OF WHITE CARDBOARD face down next to the marquee. Something told her to pick it up. Written across it in large black letters:

<u>GEORGE FADE FUNERAL 9:00 am</u>

"Nine? Fucking Nine?" She stalked to the doors, vowing not to turn on herself. This wasn't her misunderstanding or flakiness. She was clean, sober, and clear, at least about the time of the funeral.

Heat coursed up her neck as she banged through the

doors. Her anger *should* shock and bewilder these assholes. She had every right to be angry.

The service had ended. She recognized several faces from yesterday, faces now rubbernecking as she stomped down the aisle toward George's casket, horse-shoed by flower arrangements, and goddamned open, with people filing past to bid their farewells.

*Where was he?*

There. Off to the side, a pompadour inside a crowd of parishioners.

"You told me this started at ten!" Gina's voice bounced off the rafters.

The group opened as a flower, revealing its pistil, Elvis the pastor, in a different fancy black funeral suit and bolo tie. He raised his hands in a conciliatory "Let me handle the hysterical lady" way.

"Now, Gina, I did no such thing."

"You're lying. Why?" Gina spun to the surrounding parishioners, many of whom were escaping down the aisle. "Yesterday, back at the house, he told me ten a.m. *sharp*. Who even has a funeral at nine on a Saturday?"

"Gina, we all acknowledge emotions run rampant in times of sorrow," the pastor said. "You've suffered a loss. You didn't hear things proper."

The pastor's followers issued noises of agreement. His meaty hands reached for her shoulders but Gina slapped them away. Dozens of people gasped.

"Forgiveness, forgiveness." Pastor Ed raised his hands to calm the crowd. "Remember, she lost her daddy."

"If she puts her hands on you again, she's gonna lose more than that," said his wife, who today more so than yesterday could pass for a soft rock singer in an airport hotel lounge.

The pastor embraced her. "Shhh, shhh, Tawny darling."

"Take a sec and put yourself in my shoes—" Gina began, when two sandy-haired men appeared on either side of her. Must be Pastor Ed's Christian muscle. "Are you kidding me? Listen, guys, have you ever seen a crazy person go apeshit?"

No answer, of course.

Pastor Ed nodded, and the men took a few steps back from her. "There's still the service in the cemetery," he said.

"If you thought I heard nine, and if I wasn't here by nine, why not call me instead of starting without me? Help me understand, please."

"We don't have your number, dear."

"You gave me the wrong goddamn time on purpose!"

Tawny stepped forward, rouged cheeks turning magenta. "You watch your disrespect and your filthy mouth—!"

Pastor Ed seized his wife's arm. "Stop! Darlin' please. Calm it down."

Gina flexed her hands, ready to rumble if those pink-painted claws came at her. All she needed was to land a good punch between the curiously enormous boobs. The pastor swung Tawny around into a group of women who ushered her off.

He, out of breath, swept his hands through the big rip curl of his hairdo, eyes avoiding Gina's. "My deepest apologies for any confusion we may have caused. I should have written it down on a piece of paper for you. Please do join us at the cemetery." With that, he turned, enveloped by his Lambs.

Gina made a move to follow him when someone touched her arm.

## Chapter Fourteen

Mr. Beige. Freckled hand on her elbow. She fished for his name, came up empty. "Hi. What?"

"My truck is giving me trouble, so if it wouldn't be a burden, I'd be grateful for a ride up to the cemetery."

Gina's adrenaline had nowhere to go. Her limbs a bunch of useless noodles. "Do you really need a ride, or are you handling me?"

"I need a ride."

"Sure. I'll give you a lift."

"Do you have a coat?"

"In the car."

"Weather might turn. I'll grab mine. Back in a minute."

Mr. Beige strolled off to find his coat.

Gina turned in a slow circle, quietly absorbing her environment. The church had none of the bells and whistles of her mother's Catholic church. Lots of space, though, with high, airy walls unencumbered by stained glass or paintings of suffering. Several watercolors of wildflowers and holy lions. Vases in every corner stuffed with fake flowers. For all its neutral, uplifting symbology, it could be a lobby in a Scientology center.

When the crowd dispersed, the tall Native dude and the short blond man moved flowers to make a path to transport Dad to his final resting place. Gina rushed down the aisle for a last goodbye.

"Hi, again. It's me from this morning. The coffin . . . good job . . . arranging him. That was. . ."

They mumbled their hellos.

". . . like totally insane."

The older guy nodded at someone behind her, then reached for the lid.

"Hold on!"

"It's time, miss."

"Not until I'm done." She held her ground until he stepped back.

Leaning over the coffin, she told her Dad, "Sorry we didn't reconnect in person. I would have loved to learn how to play backgammon. Um, thanks for the canoe trip. And I enjoyed our calls." She lifted his black curl. The cross had been redrawn. Bigger now. "What is this for?" she asked the blond.

He approached, face squished in a frown. "Don't know. We're on a schedule, miss." The lid came down so fast it almost smacked her before she retracted her arm.

"What's wrong with you?"

"Ready." Mr. Beige was back, wrapped in a raincoat like an old-timey detective.

She debated following the men as they rolled the casket out the side door. To what end, though? More fruitless bitching?

"They didn't want me to look at him." She turned back to Mr. Beige, but he was already halfway up the aisle.

Gina dashed after the man whose name she forgot, a man whose brother spent much of the school day wiping boogers on the carpet and then died in a war, a man who'd likely asked her for a ride at the pastor's request to calm her down. Good luck with that. She pitied the poor jerk who tried to manage her mood right now.

# Chapter Fifteen

Six minutes into the ride, her passenger had said nothing beyond, "Take the Old US 40 west." More silence followed as she drove on another two-lane road bordered by prairie grass. They passed the occasional house, the Ellsworth water tank, a small prison, and a feed store. No mountains or hills on the horizon ahead.

Pressing him about the pastor's lie would increase the awkward factor tenfold. The why of the lie she'd figure out later. Plus, the more she thought about it, organized religion freaked her out, making an in-church service uncomfortable. Maybe she'd dodged a bullet. Still, their disregard irked her.

"You want to find us some music?"

He nodded, pushing presets until he landed on a Dolly Parton song.

She side-eyed him while Dolly sang about her special coat. No change in that impervious expression he wore, all pursed lips and squinty eyes.

"You don't say much, Clint Eastwood."

"I talk when I have something to say."

"But that's not your usual mode, I'm guessing. You know, asking about others. Asking them questions."

"If I have one."

"Do you ever make conversation just to be friendly?"

"Being friendly doesn't require conversation."

"How does someone convey friendliness without words? A smile? A minty green aura?"

A grin put some life in his face, which flushed her with pleasure. She fought it, refusing to betray the air of breezy casualness she was attempting to exude. However, if she were tipsy, she'd probably ram the car head-first into a hay bale and jump his beige bones.

"What do you do for a living?" she asked.

"Assistant Wastewater Treatment Plant Manager for the county."

"Ooh, my mother would say, 'A county job, very good,' and then she'd look you up and down and ask, 'Do you dance?'"

Before he answered, the song ended, and a loud commercial for a local paintball facility screamed at them. Gina turned off the radio. Silence again. Drove her nuts.

"I'm a graphic designer. I do brochures, websites, ads, and book covers. Freelance."

"Is that right?"

"Yep. Righto. Correctamundo. You betcha."

After another minute of radio silence and zero conversation, Gina blurted, "Who's paying for all this? For the funeral and the burial? Is it me? Or Dad's money? Which, God knows if there's any—

"Lamb of God."

"How?"

"Took up a collection."

"I won't be surprised by a bill?"

"Nope."

"That's very kind." Her shoulders relaxed. In fact, this guy made her feel so chill she might rip a yoga fart without embarrassment.

"I forgot your name. Sorry. I suck with names."

"Rick."

"Wait. Isn't it John, or Russ? No, it starts with a J . . . Joshua! Didn't you tell me, Joshua?"

"Rick."

"I'm positive you told me Rick died in the war."

"My brother Joshua died in the war."

"You lied?"

"Yes. Not proud for of it."

"Why?"

"Didn't want to be Rick right then. Apologies."

"Well, color me surprised. I haven't seen you pick your nose once."

A laugh escaped him. Lasted a half second. Then he tilted his head toward his side mirror. "Funeral's gonna be short."

"How come?"

"Storm."

"Jeez. It's like you people are all going 'Winter . . . is coming' when you say that."

"Your father died because of a storm."

She bristled. Apparently, jokes about Kansans declaring a weather change with an implied horror sting were off-limits and cause for shame because Dad was electrocuted by lightning. Did she have no scruples? Was this hot, nose-picking mofo chiding her?

"I wasn't judging," he said, as though privy to her thoughts. "Storms can be serious on the prairie."

"Did the lightning really travel through the phone?"

"When he picked up the landline."

She'd called Dad's cell twice, then figured he'd misplaced it, so she called the landline. And if she hadn't called the landline . . . A tingle in her fingers shot up her arms, courtesy of her tense grip on the steering wheel.

"Hey, Rick?"

"Yes?"

"I'm sorry about your brother."

"Me, too. Thank you. Oh, gosh. You want to go left on—"

"Here?" She swerved onto a smaller road, past an A-frame church building at the entrance of a big old cemetery.

Distant hills crowned by moiling clouds now became visible through the driver's side window.

"How long before it gets here?"

"I expect the ceremony will be brief."

"Is there a thing afterwards?"

"Back at Lamb of God."

"Oh gee. That sounds wonderful."

"They do a nice spread."

She guessed Nosepick Rick didn't have a nose for sarcasm.

A shimmer in the rearview drew her attention, but disappeared before she got a good look.

## Chapter Sixteen

"George was a kind man, an amusing man, a handyman," said Pastor Ed .

George was in the coffin in the hole. Gina pictured him in there, head on his stained pillow. The leaky wound.

"He was a man who struggled, as we all do—some of us more than others."

Sunflowers draped over the coffin seemed so stereotypically Midwestern to her, as did the sand-blasted color palette of the cemetery and the people in their plain Sunday clothes. Of course, she culled her ideas about the Midwestern essence from books and TV. Well, from Grant Wood paintings and *Supernatural*—the best paranormal crime-fighter series ever made. She'd watched all fifteen seasons in the last two rehabs. Something about demon-hunting hotties made it easier to keep herself from sneaking out a window to find contraband.

"Above all, George was a man who accepted Jesus Christ as his Lord and Savior and was born again."

Tawny raised her hands to Jesus. "You tell it, Ed." Her words inspired a few "Amens."

"Being born again is an immediate upending of a life directed by sin into a life of virtue, guided by faith. We all, most of us, possess this gift, do we not?" Pastor Ed pointed with his pinky-ring hand, drawing it past everyone gathered around the gravesite. "This gift of eternal life?"

Gina tensed. Everyone knew who wasn't reborn in this group.

"George found divine grace in his darkest moment, and through his acceptance of Christ, was forgiven of his sins, and is now in heaven."

Everyone, even Gina, responded with "Amens."

"Though he faltered along the way, we always got George back on track, didn't we?"

"Amen!"

"He leaves behind him a beautiful and spirited daughter." Faces swiveled to Gina. A few people murmured "Amen," as if unsure it was warranted.

Under the stress of scrutiny, Gina offered a tip-of-the-hat gesture, then giggled like a jackass before folding in on herself, squaring her shoulders and smiling vaguely at the sunflowers.

"And he left behind fond memories for many of us. From winning the hotdog eating contest at our last carnival, to his many projects for Mrs. Olson, to using his carpentry skills to upgrade our church. George truly gave back to the community that took him into their fold, as we hope we can do for his daughter."

Again with the hand. Again with the looks. Gina resented her welling tears.

Rick patted her shoulder. Was this an act of Christian charity? Or genuine affection? Or more? Was she such a wretched, horny heathen she'd speculate about his intentions at her dad's funeral?

"Personally, I remember the day George first came to me," the pastor said. "It was after a sermon on forgiveness I gave on King David, who committed adultery, then, to cover it up, had the woman's husband murdered! Adultery! Murder! How could David ever be forgiven?"

A darting movement by the old obelisks caught Gina's attention. A thin, elderly woman in black tights, black dress, black sun hat, and black sunglasses scampered between them. If someone were to play her in a movie, they'd have to CGI Bette Davis circa the mid-1970s.

"David begged, 'Have mercy on me, oh God, because of Your unfailing love. Blot out the stain of my sins.' And God did!"

CGI Bette Davis got herself a stone's throw from the coffin, sheltering behind two plump women. She cocked her head and cupped her right ear to listen. The total effect was cartoonish.

"He said to me, 'Pastor Ed, I want to give my life to Christ!'"

Gina tuned out the mourners singing "Amazing Grace" and watched CGI Bette meerkating behind the women, her attention split between the coffin and Gina. Those big black bug glasses were so disconcerting as they fixed on her, Gina sprouted goosebumps on her neck.

At the song's end, Pastor Ed handed Gina a shovel.

"Oh, right, thanks." She scooped dirt and sprinkled it on his coffin. "Bye, Dad."

Distant thunder rumbled in the distance. Or was that Dad's theatrical farewell?

"Folks, the weather is turning rotten, and I wouldn't want anybody stuck on the road when this squawker comes through," Pastor Ed said. "So, unfortunately, we must cancel today's event back at Lamb of God." At the few groans, he opened his arms as if embracing everyone. "Tell ya what: we'll serve the food tomorrow after service. George wouldn't mind that."

Gina swung her head around, finding Rick. "No food? No refreshments? Isn't that the only upside to all this?" He didn't respond, being too riveted by the weather. A tickle at her back made her turn the other way to find Pastor Ed looking at her, or Rick, or both of them.

CGI Bette had disappeared. No owlish woman in flight. If she wasn't a ghost visible only to Gina, then she had to be the unknown caller. Gina made a mental note to charge Dad's phone and call her back.

"We should go now," Rick said.

# Risk for Severe Storm

**WHERE LIGHTNING STRIKES**

Enos A. Mills in Saturday Evening Post.

I took shelter from a thunder storm in a prospector's cabin far up a mountain slope. Jerry Sullivan and I stood in the open doorway watching the breathing clouds over us and the drifting clouds in the canons below, when out of an almost clear sky came a bolt of lightning. It struck an aged fir tree and blew it as completely to fragments as though dynamited from top to bottom. Splinters and chunks of wood were showered round us. A shattered stump two feet in diameter and not more than a foot high was all that remained of the 80 foot fir. Booming and broken echoes of the crash resounded among the canons.

To camouflage my feelings I turned to Sullivan and asked, in a matter of fact manner:

"Why is it that lightning never strikes twice in the same place?"

Like lightning came the reply:

"It don't need to!"

# Chapter Seventeen

Gina plugged Dad's phone into an outlet by the microwave. After a quick survey of the half-dozen containers in the fridge, she chose a tater tot casserole. The microwave looked as old as herself, so she stood over the sink, gobbling cold tots by giant spoonfuls while staring out the kitchen window at the developing storm that had turned day to night by four p.m.

She avoided thoughts about Dad and the funeral. Rick was a better subject. He'd held her arm in the graveyard as they headed back to her car. Did they complement each other? She, dark-haired and brown-eyed, with deep shadows in her clavicles. He, a beige Chiaroscuro of freckles and flaxen highlights from his Swedish forbearers. Though his lanky stride matched hers, it had a more laconic gait to it. Belief in eternal life must comfort him. She wished she believed in anything, if only herself.

From the outside, Rick's house was modest but well-kept. A man who took care of his business. Her primary issue with him, aside from the viability of dating someone who lived halfway across America, was the evangelism. She wouldn't date a Wiccan or a Catholic or a Scientologist unless they never spoke of their doctrines. Still, that handsome bastard lodged himself in her fantasies. Most of her previous relationships began with immediate drunk sex. How tantalizing to imagine an old-fashioned sober courtship filled with modest escalations, from an innocent brush of hands to a sweet kiss, to mad necking, to frantic spooning, to full-frontal— "FUCK!"

Gina caught her reflection in the kitchen window: an exhausted glutton with rings under her eyes. In the shock of it, she'd gasped and panic-swallowed a sizable clump of tots, which then log-jammed in her throat. She hacked them into the sink, feeling the pressure in her eyes from coughing. Cold tap water sent them down the drain. She splashed water on her face and patted it with the towel she found folded on the sink. Less than a week ago, Dad had used this towel, a sodden, mildewy thing that stank of lavender dryer sheets and mold. Despite the stench, she kept her head cradled inside its hard cotton, wondering if she could nap right here at the sink, letting herself sink.

--until the snick-snick of a broom brushed across the floor behind her.

Gina straightened up but kept the towel over her eyes. An eerie sensation slewed down her back. She wasn't alone in here.

Slowly, she lowered the towel but kept her eyes on the cheesy splat in the sink. Despite every inclination not to do so, she glanced again at her reflection.

A dark figure hovered behind her.

Gina yelped and reeled around, wielding the spoon as if it would protect her against—

—an empty kitchen. Nothing in here except a hint of a breeze. Her eyes darted around searching for movement. Nobody so much as breathed, except herself. She heaved deep breaths to ensure she didn't pass out or tip over the edge into a panic attack.

A Kitchen Witch doll hung on the wall next to the pantry. Mom used to sell them at the farmer's market in Sherman Oaks but honed the craft here. Gina spent many a day helping her glue on felt hats. Had she seen but not acknowledged the doll and then, in her discombobulation, magnified it and saw it hovering behind her?

Gina dropped the towel. Stress subsided. She tapped her foot on the chipped linoleum floor. Then both feet. She syncopated the tapping and picked up speed until "Tea for Two" played in her head, along with a memory of how fun it was to tap dance with a bunch of old people in rehab.

The delightful sound of her tapping reduced the dread. She performed the complete song, even the part about baking a sugar cake, and ended the number with a fancy little ball change. Then, after a gracious curtsy to an invisible audience, out she went, assuring herself this had been a confluence of unprecedented emotions at a vulnerable time in her recovery, and she was handling it all as best she could. Yes, she was doing fine. Fine, fine, fine. All the way to the car, the positive self-talk ran through her head. *Doing as well as can be expected, Gina girl.*

She popped the trunk and dug into the airport convenience store bag for the liquid non-habit-forming over-the-counter sleep aid containing only a smidge of alcohol. The three unmeasured swigs would surely earn a cluck of disapproval from her sponsor. *Who cares.* There was only a teensy bit of alcohol. Not enough to hook her. She had to sleep, right? Sleep cured all.

A raindrop splatted on her nose, reminding her of the broken window in the parlor. She should've gotten someone to fix that stupid window. Rick would know a person. For now, she needed a tarp. But where to find a tarp?

Gina turned to the behemoth black slab of a barn.

*Damn.*

# Chapter Eighteen

Aware of something awful about the barn she couldn't nail down, Gina summoned an AA quote she'd turn to when tempted to turtle up and ignore her problems: "Winners do what they have to do, and losers do what they want to do." *Be a winner, Gina.* She turned on her phone flashlight and wound her way through the car graveyard.

Somehow, she resisted assumptions about previous owners or the absence of license plates. The cars' shadowy, often burned-out interiors were bad enough, though nothing close to the creeps she got from the danglers on the rearview mirrors. A graduation tassel here, a saint's medal there.

And now the barn. A long-ago fire had charred its edges. Probably lightning, the theme of her visit, the end of her father.

"You'd better have a tarp in there, or else!" she yelled at the barn doors. Bluster was to fear what tequila was to nagging reality. She found the small padlock key, and soon the doors puffed open, emitting a rotted wood odor. She used her elbows to push inside.

Trailing her light overhead into the rafters, she noted all the places murderous drifters might bed down. Once satisfied nobody perched up there, she inspected corners, stacks of boxes, the sit-on lawn mower, and a surfboard. Why did her Midwestern-born and bred dad own a surfboard? Moving the light along, she found an overturned canoe, stoking memories of their canoe trip and those prairie chickens.

A lump formed in her throat. She resented Dad's sudden demise, the cutoff of weekly phone calls, the thwarted Thanksgiving plans of surprising him by showing up unannounced, or the newer plan to inform him about her surprise visit so he'd have something to anticipate.

*All gone.*

Her light blew past a can of paint, then swung back to find more cans, brushes, and a plastic tarp stuffed into a cardboard box. Convinced the box teemed with creepy crawlies, she removed her coat and shirt, then put the coat back on and wrapped the shirt around her hand before picking up the box.

On her way out, she paused to stare at a claw-foot tub in the corner. Something about it froze her insides, or maybe she didn't have insides but a dark void instead of organs. A place of unimaginable emptiness. And now heat, so much heat. The emptiness ignited with flame. Every breath fed the flame. The heat became unbearable. She had to get out of there before she melted, but her feet felt stuck to the floor. It took a monumental scream in her head—*GO!*—before she moved.

She kicked the doors closed behind her, didn't bother

locking them, and had nearly reached the house when she heard banging sounds.

"What the hell now?" She set the box down and jogged back to the barn. On her third trip through the car graveyard she'd become inured to its eerie landscape. She shut and locked the barn doors, then hurried back and picked up the box, when the noise started up again. She swung her light down the side of the house. Ah. The doors to the storm cellar were open, lifting and dropping in the wind.

*Thump . . . thump . . . thump . . .*

Sighing, she approached the doors. Her journey across the dark yard punctuated by bright lightning pulses. Recollections of what she thought she saw in the parlor kept her jaw firmly clenched. The sky popped bright with false daylight.

The Kitchen Witch's shadow was walking up the stairs from the cellar.

Both she and it straightened up at the sight of the other.

"Jesus!" Gina dropped the phone and the box. "Shit! Phone!" She fell to her knees, hands spidering across the damp ground as distant thunder drummed closer.

On the next lightning strobe, she found her phone and jumped to her feet. At another, she risked a glance at the cellar. The shadow had disappeared, and the doors were shut. What kind of shadow shows up in direct light, anyway? Was this a human? A black mass? A black hole? Theories reeled through her lizard brain as she broke personal speed records hauling ass back inside, forgetting that being in the house promised no respite from uncanny shit.

Once inside, Gina flipped the deadbolt behind her, dropped the tarp box, and ran to the door she feared most as a child: cellar access from the kitchen. If a spooky shadow were floating around downstairs, she wanted to lock the barrel bolt. Didn't matter if non-corporeal ghoulies could vaporize and pour through cracks and keyholes. The hitch of the lock provided lukewarm comfort.

She dragged the tarp into the parlor and spread it out under the broken window. It wouldn't keep the floor totally dry, but might prevent additional water damage.

The best strategy here and now would be to locate the duffle and car keys and rent a motel room in town. But what about the house? All the stuff? She'd at least have to find Dad's important papers. As she wavered, the OTC sleep aid hit her with the force of a five-hundred-pound feather pillow. There'd be no driving tonight.

Tomorrow, she'd find all the important papers and split first thing she told herself before hustling outside to the Hyundai. Fear of the shadow thing perched on her hood lingered, despite humming "Tea for Two." She got into the passenger seat and adjusted the seat back, so none of the car mirrors would reflect the outside cellar doors or the barn or any of the house windows. Soon, rain hammered the roof. On sleepless nights in Los Angeles she'd play rain sounds on YouTube. The real thing wasn't as soothing. A half hour passed without sleep, even though she listed the states in her head again and again.

Eventually, the storm moved west, revealing the full moon. So lovely. So comforting. Whether waking up on a bus in San Francisco, or in Disneyland jail, or real jail, whatever the misadventure, she always found the moon for proof of life, for the promise of a tomorrow to pick herself up and try again.

She turned to her other side. Glanced at the car clock. 10:33 p.m. Wow. She must have fallen asleep after all. It wasn't too late to call the West Coast. She raised her phone, pressed "Mom." Mom loved the moon, and since moving to the new place, always gave Gina updates on its phase, position, and color.

After four rings, a voice of warm honey answered. "Hello, darling girl."

"Full moon, with a slight orange cast."

"The colors of the prairie."

"He kept the Kitchen Witch."

"Aw . . . my witches . . .my kitchen. . ."

Gina waited for more, but Mom trailed off into nonsense words.

"Did I tell you about the drawing of George the First in the courtroom?"

"Is it late where you are, Gina Ballerina?"

"Not really. Can you talk?"

"Sure."

"The picture changed, Mommy. The picture of my great- or great-great—I don't know how many greats of a grandfather. But turns out he was a murderer."

"Are you in bed now?"

"Kind of. Hard to keep my mind off all this insanity. Did you hear what I just said?"

"Gina Ballerina, my Kitchen Witch will look after you."

"Um. I know you mean for that to sound comforting, Mom, but Jesus."

Mom's laughter serenaded her as Gina dipped into unconsciousness. Not even the nearby lightning flashes could rouse her.

# Chapter Nineteen

Sunshine flared across Gina's eyelids until she jerked awake to the new day with a crick in her neck and a dead cell phone. The car clock told her it was 9:05 a.m. She'd slept for over ten hours.

After a quick debate about leaving, quitting, letting the state of Kansas have everything, the need for money won out and inside she went. She estimated a good nine hours to accomplish before the sun dropped.

Her first stop was the room she slept in. The diary was on the bed. The last time she saw the diary, it was on the floor, or was it the nightstand? These memory lapses, once a common occurrence, had stopped when she got sober. So then why—?

She pushed away fearful thoughts and dug through her duffel, pulling out a Rebel T7 camera. She hung it around her head, then went into the junk room to investigate the desk. To her surprise, the file drawer contained a tidy arrangement of hanging green file holders with manila folders inside, labeled: House, Car, Insurance, Will, Bank. *Wow.* She'd imagined an all-day excavation into a mountain of receipts and ancient bank statements, but Dad had some mad organizational skills.

In the back of the drawer hung a folder labeled "Gina." Memories of Dad didn't square with its contents. Here were school pictures from fourth grade through high school, along with copies of report cards and printed pages of her website, including work samples. All these years of distrust, and turns out he had regrets and perhaps waited for her to reach out. By the time she did, it was too late.

Snapping her thoughts shut along with the folder, she switched her focus to coffee. Succor for the tired and unmotivated. Downstairs, she plonked her duffel by the door and Dad's folders on his TV tray by the recliner, then made coffee with grounds she brought from her favorite Sherman Oaks coffee shop. She plugged the phone into a kitchen outlet, then dragged the pot of rainwater sitting in a pool of its overflow to the kitchen door and poured it down the stone steps.

Marveling at the timelessness of the wild grass and the old clothesline, she pointed and clicked in every direction. The big yard was perfect for a family. If it were anywhere near Los Angeles County, she'd net fifteen times what she'd get for it in Kansas. No memories connected to the yard. Nothing felt familiar.

Back in the kitchen she found a mop in a bucket in the pantry's corner. Dad hadn't used it much, judging by the stinky clump of congealed yarn. As she dithered on whether it would do anything beyond spreading mold, her eyes—in the way a mighty eagle spots a field mouse from six hundred yards—shifted to the pantry's corner, to a large milk crate covered with a checkered dishcloth.

"Please don't be what I know you are." She tapped its edge with her foot. Bottles clanked in confirmation of Dad's liquor, gathered and stored for easy access. She pulled up the cloth to confirm. Yup. Packed together in a one-stop shop of an alcoholic's trigger were bottles of whiskey, vodka, tequila, scotch, gin, white rum, dark rum, sweet rum, and wine.

Each fall off the wagon had sprung from curiosity seeds to cheating first in her heart. Who said that? The Bible? In her heart, she'd already finished the whiskey, started on the vodka, promising herself this was it, the last time, hand to God. It took tremendous effort to throw the cloth back over the bottles. Proud of herself, if shaky, this would make a good story for a future meeting.

Her thoughts circled over the bottles even while she swabbed the spilled rainwater with a roll of paper towels. That blue and white dishcloth reminded her of a picnic blanket. Terrific. Her weaknesses, stronger than her strengths, always lurked in the periphery, ready to fuck up her life on repeat.

She spent the next few minutes pacing the kitchen as she mulled the possibility of calling her sponsor, Bella, who might set her on a good track and calm her down. No. Bella was judgmental and scolding—two things she didn't need right now.

With no other tools or helpers at her disposal, she settled for a cup of coffee and a mantra. *You are sober. You enjoy being sober. Air is sweeter. Eyes are clearer. Mind is sharper.*

Gina unplugged Dad's phone, now showing a 35% charge, and wandered into the living room to sit in his La-Z-Boy, its smell a subtler version of his bedroom. She found the last call number and pressed the talk button. Who was the unknown caller, and what was Gina supposed to be wary of? Well, now she'd find out. As the phone rang, the familiar feeling of nervous excitement raced through her, same as when she stood up to speak at a meeting or made amends with someone who held a grudge. A computerized voice asked her to leave a message.

"Hi, this is Gina Fade. You called for my dad, George Fade. That's . . . he was my father. I think I saw you at the cemetery. Please call me. You have my number. Well, you have Dad's number. My Dad. George Fade. Thanks."

While awaiting a call back, Gina investigated some of Dad's papers. His life insurance policy would net her a hundred grand, which, along with the house and selling all the vintage crap, would either buy her a down payment on a condo in the high desert or keep her in an apartment in LA for eighteen months while she rebuilt her business.

She spent the next hour taking pictures of TV Guide covers. She'd gotten to May 20, 1961, with the adorable headline of "A Housewife's Hectic Whirl on a Quiz Show," when the phone rang.

# Chapter Twenty

Gina dashed across the room to answer. "Hi, hi, this is Gina Fade." The following three seconds of silence felt closer to ten.

"You called me, young lady," came the same sexless, graveled voice of a chain smoker.

"Hi, yes, how do you—how did you know my dad?"

"I'm Amy. Amy Fade. Aunt Amy."

"Wow. I have an aunt?

"Well, it no longer matters I suppose. If truth's to be told, I'm your grandmother."

"Whaaaa?" Gina dropped ass into the recliner. Head cocked as she solved the puzzle. Caffeine helped her do it fast. "You got pregnant as a teenager and gave birth to Dad, who your parents raised as your much younger brother?"

Another raspy breath. "Yes."

"How old were you? Did my dad know?"

"Sixteen. He did not."

"Were you at the gravesite yesterday?"

"I was."

How sad it must've been for Amy to see her son buried.

Gina waited for elaboration. But there was only a slight wheezing every few seconds. Did everyone around here run at half-speed?

"Okay. I'd like to meet you, Amy. How about helping me sort out this big mess of a house? I'm sure you'll find stuff you want to keep."

Three sharp and precise knocks at the front door jolted Gina to her feet.

"Amy. Is that you at the door?"

"Hand to the Lord, I'll never set foot on that property again."

"Why? The dead have risen? There's a curse? Sacred burial grounds? What?"

Gina edged closer to the door. The visitor switched from knuckles to the rooster-shaped cast iron door knocker.

"Amy, hold on a sec. Someone's—"

"Meet me at the cemetery today at twelve-thirty." With that, she hung up.

Now the doorbell chimed wheezily. Gina peeked through the curtains. Rick!

Mister tall drink of water stood inches from the door, holding a brown paper grocery bag with handles. He caught her gawking and shot her a stilted smile, half genuine pleasure, half mortification, a hundred percent adorable. Gina opened the door and gave him a "please enter" gesture. He didn't move.

"Okay." She joined him outside. "How was church?"

Good."

"And the food? Was there pie?"

"Mulberry."

"Dad had—we have mulberries. My mom made jam one summer." Spellbinding conversation. "So, what brings you here, Rick?"

"I brought a list of names and numbers. Could be useful." He handed her a folded paper. "The lawyer is up top. Mord Fairweather. Thought he'd be most pertinent."

"Mord. What's that short for?"

"Mordecai."

"Right." She ran her eyes down at least twenty names and numbers. "Thorough. Thank you. I found some of Dad's papers but hadn't gotten to the lawyer yet. Oh yes! A window company. I need a window. Hey, you're on here, too."

She glanced up at those hazel-amber eyes.

"If you need us."

"Us?"

"Me, 'n' Ed and the guys."

"I doubt I'll need Ed and the guys." Gina tucked the paper under her bra strap. Rick's eyes stayed locked on her boots. "Do you want some coffee? It'll slap you around and get you moving."

"No, thanks, I'm expected back at the church for clean-up. They sent me with leftovers." He held out the grocery bag.

"Ooh! Pie?"

"Yes, and casserole."

"You people are trying to kill me with casserole, aren't you? Death by cream of mushroom soup. Ba-dum-tsh."

No reaction from Rick, except a nod to the car graveyard. "I can help with those. Gosh, that could bring in a nice profit. I know a guy who's always been interested in buying the whole deal. Made George a fair offer a few years back."

This was the most speaking she'd heard from him. Perhaps his nasty attraction to her conflicted with his faith. Or was it simple Christian charity and an interest in vintage cars?

"Sounds interesting. I'll get my game plan together and be in touch."

Rick made eye contact. "Gina."

"Rick."

"Don't throw the bag away until you go through it."

"What bag, Rick?" Gina jiggled the bag. "This bag?" He nodded. "Thank you, Rick." She pictured how he'd look in bed in the morning. "Remember when your uncle drove a bunch of us to Braum's for ice cream over in Salina?" He dropped his chin, nodding bashfully. "And he let you hood surf. The moon must've been behind us because we saw your shadow on the road. A surfer shadow, arms out and everything. Even when your uncle floored it, you held on until he punched the brakes and you flew off, landing on your ass and bouncing down the road like a rock skipping across water."

"I still have the cartoon you drew of it."

"Aw, really?"

"I burned it."

"Please accept my belated apology for laughing."

"I—that was a joke."

"So you kept it?" Her skin tingled at his shy nod. "Framed? On your wall? With a light under? Or over? Either way is cool."

"It's in an old album."

"You'll have to show it to me sometime."

He subtly checked his watch, the way therapists do when end-time draws near.

"Think I could bum a smoke from you, Rick?"

As always, it felt intimate. The seductive slide of the coffin nail from its packet. Pulling it out with her lips. Waiting for him to strike the match, then cup his hand around the tip to shield it from the breeze. Her hand on his wrist. Lingering eye contact as she took a drag. His lips blowing out the flame.

"Before you head back to church, can you help me with a little something?"

"Sure."

"Inside."

"Oh?"

"It's heavy, and I need a strong helper."

He smirked at the obvious flattery and followed her to the kitchen.

"It's hard to function peacefully with these things calling to me in devil voices." She pulled the cloth off the crate of liquor. "'Gina, drink me, drink me! Wreck your life again!'"

Without a word, Rick lifted with his legs and marched the crate out of the kitchen.

"Thanks. Want me to take your ciggies away?"

"Not yet. They're not calling to me in the devil voices."

Another joke! She ran ahead to hold the front door open.

"Oh, hey, what do you know about my great-grandfather?"

"Nothing," he said. Too quick.

"Well, I think he was a bad person."

"You don't say?" He backed away from her, stoic expression fastened tightly.

"Yeah. I found a newspaper article and he. . ."

Rick's face broke out in a sheen of sweat. Sobriety had restored her acknowledgement of social cues, and though it killed her to do so, she dropped the subject.

"Call if you need something." His head knocked into the wind chimes. "All this estate business you can do from California, you know."

"Okay, I'll . . . Bye. Thanks again." How confusing. Sparks had ricocheted between them, yet he urged her to leave.

She waited until he was a trace of road dust before she dug into the bag. Fingers reaching beyond the stacked Tupperware containers until they touched a thick envelope.

Someone had written "Gina Incidentals" in Sharpie on the front. Inside, she counted six hundred and seventy dollars. "Thank you, Lambs." She stuffed the envelope into her ass pocket and went back inside.

The moment she closed the door, her eyes ziplined over to Dad's TV tray because something had changed.

## Chapter Twenty-One

The diary rested on top of his folders. "Fuck."

The newspaper article peeked out like a bookmark. Around her, the air rustled with—what? Her own tension? Something else? It felt like a glitter bomb had gone off, and now minuscule glitter bits tickled down on her exposed skin. Still, she took a step closer and reached for the diary, determined to confirm an unwelcome theory.

As certain as taxes, as dawn, as dusk, as a red light when you want a green, as rain when you forget your umbrella, as regret, as death in the end, the courtroom sketch had changed again. It'd started with George sitting inside the witness box in profile, then to a frontal depiction of his face fixated on her, and now, standing.

Time to go.

Her brain crackled. *Get your phone!* Gina bounded upstairs, grabbed her phone and bag. The only sounds were her footfalls and unruly breathing. Back downstairs she headed for the door. Then stopped. The sight in the parlor locked her feet up like a shopping cart straying off the property.

A massive pile of TV Guides formed a loose pyramid in the middle of the room. Try as she did to frame this logically, there was no imaginable way the small stacks she'd been making after photographing the covers had fallen together in this permutation on their own.

*Okay.*

Either ghosts were real and wanted her gone, or a phrogger lived in the attic and snuck out to scare her off. At the crawly feeling of her nerve endings tightening she had to make her next move. She clocked the nooks and crannies for possible cameras or tiny holes through which a creeper might observe her. Nothing jumped out. Thankfully.

*Be cool.*

If she broke down into babbling hysterics, she lost advantage—akin to buying an eight-ball from a guy named Squidgie who open-carried in Riverside and might have also been a pimp. You don't let Squidgie see your fear. You walk in with the attitude of someone who isn't above rabbit-punching balls.

Without a plan she stalked over to the stairs and shouted up at the attic-access panel on the landing, "I know you're in there, asshole! I know what you're doing! I'm calling the cops!"

Nothing and nobody ran off or flew off or cackled maniacally. On to the kitchen, where she yelled, "Get the fuck out" at the cellar door, before moving to the parlor where she intended to issue another threat. Except here, the strange buzzing energy she'd been experiencing attacked her full force. The shelves where the TV Guides once lived were empty—but for a single book standing on the highest shelf. She moved closer to read the title on its spine.

*Oh, the Places You'll Go!*

The Dr. Seuss book Dad used to read to her at night!

After Mom tucked her in, he'd scoot in bed next to her with his dirty work boots dangling off the end of the bed. Gina would imagine where the boots took him throughout the day. If she asked, he'd concoct a silly tale about climbing the Eiffel Tower, or jet-packing down the Smoky River, or chasing the varmint chickens who stole his lunch. *Wow*. A good memory. Damn lump in her throat. Real human feelings again instead of desperate impulses. *Whatever*. She wouldn't include the book in an estate sale.

She reached for it but pulled away when a twinge of static electricity ran up her hand. Then it flew off the shelf and dropped onto the floor next to her.

In the presence of the uncanny, some people scream; others lose their minds. Gina stayed quiet, hoping a non-reaction might stave off whatever madness waited for a tipping point before revealing itself.

The book had landed open on the first page, to the image of the little boy in his yellow jumper and beanie cap. It read: *Congratulations! Today is your day. You're off to Great Places! You're off and away!*

Gina bit the inside of her cheek to keep her teeth from chattering.

Why this page? Was it random?

As an answer, the pages fanned to the final page, where the little boy rode off in a hot-air balloon to his next adventure. *Today is your day! Your mountain is waiting, so get on your way!*

A phrogger couldn't have done this unless they also had telekinesis. An intelligent, invisible being had delivered a message via a trope straight out of the many horror films Gina watched compulsively in rehab.

And so Gina got on her way.

But in her haste, she left behind Dad's papers.

# Chapter Twenty-Two

Unrelenting waves of heat followed by cold winds blew through her as she entertained boundless, unanswerable questions about the house. So engrossed in her internal chaos, Gina would be hard-pressed to recount her journey to the cemetery beyond obeying GPS directions.

Upon seeing the cemetery gates, Gina emerged from her autopilot state and took the left fork to Dad's burial site. It wasn't long before a slender figure in a gray poncho, black capri pants, and a long, black neck scarf appeared from behind a small tomb and scampered across the grass, waving at her like a wraith in a silent movie, except for the familiar buggy sunglasses of Bette Davis in her hagsploitation years. *Amy*.

Amy then stepped in front of her car, forcing Gina to stomp the brake.

"Jesus Christ, old woman!"

Amy came around to the driver's side window. Motioned for Gina to roll it down.

"You're late." A starburst of wrinkles radiated out from bright red lips wrapped around a cigarette.

"Hello. Grandma? Aunty? Aunty Grandma?"

"Amy will do." Smoke plumed from her mouth.

Gina got out. "What are we doing? Should we visit Dad —George?"

"Let's not wait till the cows come home." Amy started up the grass, her sharp nose pointed north as though sniffing her way to the gravesite. "Do you remember me, girl?"

"Nope."

"I remember you. Always hiding in your momma's skirts. Shy when folks were looking, naughty when they weren't."

"That's a lovely tribute. Thank you, Amy."

"An observation, not a compliment."

"I'm going to pretend it was a compliment, though."

"Are you a comedian?"

"Not that I'm aware of."

"Your father made jokes."

"Right."

Gina noticed a few other "Fade" graves as they neared Dad's.

"Gina. Not Georgina? Or Regina? Never asked your folks. I expect you were named after my grandmother, Gina, short for Luigiana. She came from Italy."

"Yeah, just Gina."

"Poor Gina."

"Me?"

"No, Luigiana."

"Why? What happened? Are you going to tell me something that'll ruin my life? I'm kidding. But are you?"

"I got five minutes before I have to leave, for reasons I will inform ya of."

Amy stopped at the pile of wilting sunflowers and fresh dirt. "You were a nice little girl. Your arrival was an occasion of joy."

"People have always said that about me."

Gina felt Amy's withering look behind her shades.

"I know you are an unchurched young woman, so what I am about to tell you might be hard to comprehend." Her veiny hand darted beneath her scarf and poncho and emerged with a rosary. "I will not judge you or your upbringing. Churchgoing is no measure of the pious. Even demons can attend church. Understand?"

"Not in the least."

"Well, try, girl." Those bug glasses locked on the grave as she spoke. "You need to learn about the family curse."

Oh, so she *was* going to tell her something that might ruin her life.

"The demon lives in lightning. If you're struck direct, you die. If you survive, it crawls inside ya and pulls your strings."

Gina had too many questions to ask even one.

"After George was hanged, it got my grandmother. Poor Gina. She lived. And when she began speaking Latin, which she'd never known before, the doctors said it must be a forgotten memory. She began biting people, and the doctors called it old age. Eventually, she died of a stroke. Poor Gina."

"It possessed them?"

"It struck my poppa on a picnic, and he died. Cancer spared my momma. I escaped before it noticed me. Your daddy wasn't so lucky. It hunted him for years. One day, when you were a toddler, it found him out by the barn. He survived. But he was changed. Spent hours in the barn. Or disappeared for days. Cars showed up in the yard without explanation. He shaved off serial numbers, stripped the license plates. Brought home several bikes to boot."

The mention of cars and bikes flip-flopped Gina's heart. How many abandoned cars were in the car graveyard, and how many bikes were in that extra room?

"What are you telling me, Amy? About Dad? This is freaking me out."

"Facts, girl. The church helped cast it out, and with their continued help, Georgie hid from it for years, until his will weakened. He got caught this time. My poor Georgie." Her voice quivered. Poor Amy. "I tried to rescue him but failed." Amy crossed herself and tucked the rosary back under her scarf. "Been praying for forgiveness ever since."

"Why did they draw a cross on his forehead?"

"Do you have cicadas out by the sea?"

"Sure."

"They burrow into the ground and wake up years later. When . . . it . . . wakes up . . . I think those church lunatics believe a cross locks it inside the vessel. And they might not be wrong. There were a few upset graves and whatnots with my grandfather and grandmother."

Gina pictured lightning emerging from Dad's mouth.

At the gnarr of distant thunder, the bug glasses turned east to where clouds congregated over the low hills.

"We should go." Amy dropped her stub of a cigarette, squished it into the grave dirt with a ballet flat, then nodded for Gina to follow her back to the car.

"Don't trust the church, girl. That pastor—his sister disappeared twenty-odd years ago, and the boy got to be a warrior for Jesus, although not in the way of being *as* Jesus, merciful and whatnot."

"I can't . . . I'm trying—"

"Fix all this in your brain however you please, so long as

you leave. Go back to California." "Or"—she unlocked a vintage white Lincoln Continental—"I got a sewing room I never use with a fine trundle bed. You can settle the estate from there. Stay safe and so forth."

"How is your place safer?"

"Outside its hunting grounds."

"What?"

"Every predator has its territory."

"I need to hide?"

"Perhaps not. If it hasn't seen you."

*Uh oh.*

Gina dug the camera out of her purse as Amy lit another cigarette.

"Here."

She held the camera in front of Amy. On it was the picture of George Fade, the first snarling by the witness box. Amy's mouth fell open, and the cigarette dropped.

"How dare you put that creature before my eyes!" She practically jumped into her car.

"Is that what you meant about him seeing me?"

"Follow me home now."

"Where's 'there'?"

Amy lowered the passenger-side visor, spilling her keys onto the seat, where a small pistol sat atop a large manila envelope.

"Outside Topeka. About a hundred fifty miles east as a crow flies."

Regardless of the gun or the fact that this old lady was probably batshit, Gina was about to say "yes" when she remembered what she left behind.

"Crap! I forgot Dad's papers. Can we stop by the house to get—?"

Amy shook her head so vehemently, her sunglasses almost fell off.

"Okay. I'll go grab the papers and then drive to your place."

Amy slid out the envelope from beneath the pistol and handed it to her. "Read the pages as soon as you can. They're from an old diary, and they'll show ya I'm not crazy. I know you got those thoughts. My address is on the envelope."

Gina glanced. Amy lived in Auburn, Kansas.

"If you choose to be foolhardy and not come, stay inside. Don't pick up the land phone. Don't use appliances or run a bath or even sit on the toilet while it's about. And don't get too close to the windows."

"Ooh, it's coming to get us right now?" Gina's sarcasm, as always, functioned as the tarp stretched across her sinkhole of anxiety.

"No, girl, it's coming for *you*."

# It Comes for You

**Deaths From Lightning**

Fear of lightning is one of man's oldest emotions. Prehistoric man feared lightning as the weapon of unseen spirits. All of the old mythologies made lightning the servant of the chief god. The Greeks for example gave the thunderbolt to Zeus.

Records tell us that both Julius Caesar and Napoleon were afraid of lightning. It is not difficult to understand their fear. They felt themselves the equal of all earthly foes but the lightning out of the sky was something against which they could not defend themselves.

# Chapter Twenty-Three

Amy's throaty Lincoln beeped as it passed her car, but Gina, immersed in the missing diary pages, failed to notice.

*June 25, 1924.*

*Thoughts on the tragic death of my best friend, Tom, whose funeral I attended yesterday. Once I document my experience on these pages, I will hide them, because both Papa and Mother snoop. They dislike Tom's family and call his parents heathens because they grow herbs and do not attend church.*

*The morning was hot and winds blew light and steady. It was a perfect day for kiting. I ate my porridge on the porch so I could watch for Tom's signal. Since his house was west of ours, he used the east rising sun and his mother's hand mirror to send the signal. I was happy when I saw its glimmer, for it meant Tom could spend the day kiting.*

*After chores, we met in our regular spot out at the mud hut we made last spring. We called it The Fort and nobody knew about it but us and some rabbits.*

*Tom brought a can of beer he stole from his father and we*

*passed it back and forth until it was empty. My head felt as hot and cloudy as the day itself. He told me his ma and pop sent him to bed early the night before. They lit a small fire behind the barn, killed a chicken, and used its blood for something I will not commit to paper, even knowing these pages will never be read.*

*At the river, we ran to get our kites aloft. Mine held up in the wind. Tom's had so many ribbons on the tail it got too heavy to sustain. He kept at it for nearly an hour before the winds blew fast enough to keep his kite in the air. I staked mine so I could lie down on the grass and watch it dance in the breeze.*

*The storm came in fast. Clouds travelled from the north and the south until they met over the river in a loud thunderclap. Until then, neither of us had cause for alarm. We grew up here, and we knew how fast the weather could turn.*

*I had staked my kite, so I stepped on the tether to reduce the tension, then pulled it down, hand over hand, as fast as I could without breaking my skin. Tom's kite flew wild as he wound the spool. By the time I had mine in hand, Tom was still fighting his.*

*Day became night, except in those moments when lightning filled the sky. The first bolt struck a tree about three hundred yards to the East. I yelled to Tom to let the kite go. He told me he had worked too hard to lose his kite to a storm.*

*What I then witnessed has diminished my faith in Christ and the church. I no longer have the comfort of believing that God protects us.*

*Inside the largest cloud, a darkness spun until it became a figure. It pushed against the edges like a chick trying to break its shell. I yelled at Tom to follow me to the fort. I must have run two hundred feet before I noticed he wasn't behind me. Then I heard a great crash.*

*In the sky above me, a shape emerged from a hole in the cloud. It had a pointed head and glowing eyes. It tore the cloud in two. The ground vibrated. I had seen a similar creature in a book I found at Tom's house. It looked to be half-dragon, half-human. It was darker than the storm itself.*

*The clouds became wings that created winds so strong they swept me off my feet. I dropped my kite and tumbled across the grass.*

*I told Tom to hurry. He didn't respond and still would not let go of his kite.*

*The creature soared to earth. Its arms were lightning bolts. They reached for Tom. A pointy finger touched the kite. I swear to Jesus and Mary, I heard it laugh. The lightning burned the ribbons all the way down the string to Tom's hands. Soon his body was covered in flames.*

*Tom floundered and screamed as the flames spread across his body. Mercifully, the clouds dropped rain, which doused the fire. His body looked melted in places and burnt in varying shades of pink and red. His open eyes shone with blue fire. I believed him dead until his mouth twitched in an attempt to speak. I leaned in to listen. He had bitten off the end of his tongue. The piece of it was on the grass beside him, burnt almost to ashes. Tom's fingers had blackened, too. Their flesh curled from the bones like charcoal flowers.*

*His last words were, "I see you now." A bolt of lightning struck out from his body and disappeared into the sky. I felt my skin prickle in the current. Blood gushed from Tom's mouth as the blue fire went out.*

*I found this passage in Ezekiel 1:4, almost as if my hands directed me to the exact page: "And I looked, and behold, a whirlwind came out of the north, a great cloud, and a fire infolding itself, and a brightness was about it, and out of the midst thereof as the color of amber, out of the midst of the fire."*

*As always, I turn to the bible. It is with a sad heart I confess to finding no comfort in its content, for it does not dispel the terror of Tom's final words, or of the creature with its eyes boring into mine. I dread the day I get caught in a storm, and it comes for me.*

## Chapter Twenty-Four

"Bye, Dad."

Gina coasted under the cemetery's iron archway, knowing she'd never return. He'd been a ghost to her long before he died.

*Its arms were lightning bolts.*

She transitioned to Highway 14 going south.

*His body covered in flames.*

Six miles to go. Winds held steady. She might need gas before heading to Auburn.

*All those blue-eyed dads in her childhood drawing.*

She turned on the radio, irrationally hoping to hear some Puppenfabrik, but settled for country oldies. Her mind skipped between upcoming tasks such as selling cars and collectibles, draining the bank account, getting the place appraised, and how she'd accomplish it all from Auburn, Kansas. Whenever her brain brought up the pyres of TV Guides, she hummed "Tea for Two," and course-corrected back to how she'd make money from all of this.

*Bones like charcoal flowers.*

By the time she got to Dad's, sunshine peeked through

pinholes in the cloud cover. She left the door open as she raced inside, ready for a quick grab-and-go. She headed straight for the TV tray.

Stopped.

Rather, her body stopped. This was becoming a habit.

Someone was inside the house with her. She'd felt it several times, this sense of being observed. Would she duck in time if all the TV Guides flew at her?

*Move, Gina.* She continued to the TV tray, tossed the diary onto the recliner, collected the stack of folders and Dad's cell, and moved toward the door, not running, but not dawdling. Her arms and feet tingled.

The door slammed in her face.

Undaunted, she reached for the doorknob.

The deadbolt *clicked and* locked.

"Stop!"

She unlocked it.

*CLICK.*

Gina reeled around, ran for the kitchen. Curtains swayed. The flat-panel TV trembled on the antique below it. The Jesus and Gina pictures jittered across the mantel. Earthquake?

No.

Thunderclaps boomed loud as five-hundred-foot tidal waves crashing onto rocks. This wasn't an earthquake but a big bastard of a storm.

She shot out the back door, jumped off the steps, and rounded the house, piloting on instinct and adrenaline. Into the Hyundai. Folders tossed into the back seat. Engine revved.

Then, and only then, did she look up.

A massive tarantula of pitch-black clouds perched over the house.

Eight legs undulated in ropy tornado funnels. Suggestions of inky lines approximated a face, with two tiny blue dots for eyes. Another eye opened. Then another, until dozens of blue dots pointed at her.

*His eyes shone with blue fire.*

Gina wrenched the shifter into reverse and sped down the twisty driveway.

The creature reared back and hopped over the house in pursuit.

Gina bumped off the edges of the driveway, flattening grass and churning mud.

The sky bled in torrents, strobed with electricity. Four feet of visibility. The wipers didn't help. She pitched blindly onto the highway with zero control. Tires met the wet road and lost their grip, hydroplaning the Hyundai across both lanes.

Gina gripped the wheel but eased off the gas, fighting the urge to punch the brakes as the car freewheeled. Goddamn, it was gaining on her! She held her breath until the tires gripped again, then fought the wheel, steered back into her lane, and slammed the accelerator to the floor. She hadn't a clue whether she was heading in the direction of Amy's home.

The thing behind her belched thunder and spat fire.

Gina flipped on the brights and the defroster and turned the wipers to high. *Eyes on the road, Gina.* Still, she checked the rearview mirror.

A spider leg coiled into a strike position.

*SNAP!*

As the right rear tire exploded, the car hitched and dropped closer to the ground. Gina tightened her grip on the wheel.

A rolling thunderclap resolved into "*Gee-nuh.*"

"Fuck you!" A speed check clocked her at fifty-seven. The car could handle ninety, but not in the rain on a bare rim.

Another strike! Another tire gone. The car again strayed across the dividing line. Gina fought the wheel. This time it won. She remembered reading somewhere that you should go limp if you're going to fall or hit something. Where did she read that?

She screamed for her mother as she careened into nothing, toward nothing, seeing nothing, bracing for impact but trying to keep her body loose. *It was in an article in a woman's magazine I read in line at the market.* Drunks survive crashes because they're too loose for catastrophe to break their bones. Wouldn't it be so, so Gina to die while sober when being drunk might've spared her?

She released the wheel and covered her face. The car shuddered over roadside rumble strips before plunging nose-first into a drainage ditch.

## Chapter Twenty-Five

Gina's hands shielded her head from slamming into the steering wheel. Every muscle in her body tensed, awaiting ambush. Would death come fast or protracted? Minutes passed. Nothing happened, just the minor calamity of a shaken young woman in a car in a ditch filled with mud.

The rain reduced to a gentle drizzle, and the windshield cleared enough to see insinuations of sunlight through thinning clouds.

But none of this shit mattered now because Yannick had left behind the itty-bitty Jack Daniel's bottles and there they sat on the passenger-side floor. Roadside copulation must have made him forgetful. JD. The Jackie D. Two Jackie D's. She imagined the velvety heat trickling down her throat and reached over for them and squeezed them tight.

*Oh God. I'm a piece of shit. I'm a horrible piece of shit.* Recriminations before the act.

As a weak compromise, she dropped one bottle into the empty coffee holder. Some bizarro logic dictated she shouldn't blow two months of sobriety with *two* little boozes. Yep, the muscle memory of justifications and bargaining returned without a hiccup. The excuses she'd make to fail. After all, she survived an accident. Anybody facing this utter madness would need a drink. When she was safe and the sun appeared unburdened by menacing clouds, she'd never touch a drop ever again.

Gina used her teeth to twist off the cap. The stinging caramel scent triggered a drool response. *Don't think. Drink.*

So she did.

1.7 ounces of silky, smoky nectar. A mini. A nip. A belt. A swill. A slug. A swig. She'd have to shitcan her gold sixty-day chip. She let the bottle drop on the floor and leaned back, fighting the urge to bash her head against the steering wheel.

"Alabama, Alaska . . ." *Drink the other bottle. No.* "Arizona, Arkansas, California . . ."

Drizzle lightened to a soft mist, through which the bright lights of Gunnar's Gas & Groceries glowed at her from a quarter mile down the road. Surreal comfort of civilization beaming through the fog. Close enough to risk a drive on bare rims. But two tires gone meant only two tires left to insulate the car from an electrical strike.

"Colorado, Connecticut, Delaware . . ." She'd determine whether to drive down the swale alongside the road or go on foot when she turned the key. The car started! Decision made.

She banged on the steering wheel in victory, shifted to Drive and got the car leveled out, traveling about five feet before it sputtered to a stop. "Come on!" She felt like a sitting duck, stuck in the car, entertaining insane thoughts of being cocooned in a web, body inert and numb as a creature crept closer and closer.

*Do something, Gina.*

Eyeballing horizons ahead and behind provided welcome solace. The sky had cleared, with no webbing or spider storm in sight. She stuck her head out the window. Damn. The tires were stuck. She started the engine again. The front tire rotated uselessly, splattering her face with red mud. She laughed for a minute straight, nothing in her head but how she probably looked like one of those women in *The Descent* when they emerged from the mud pool with madness in their eyes. A woman made feral by the trauma of an inexplicable new reality.

She calmed down out of necessity. The laughter had begun to hurt her possibly broken ribs. Her phone sat on the passenger-side floor with the rest of what used to be inside her purse. It held a charge of 18%. Who would she call? Mom? No.

She pulled the paper out of her bra, and with the kind of twitchy, inept fingers she got in dreams, she tried texting Rick. There was too much to say. She gave up with a sigh and pushed Call.

"Delaware, Florida, Georgia, Hawaii, Idaho, Illinois, Indiana—"

It went straight to voicemail. "This is Rick. Leave your message at the tone."

"Hi. It's Gina. Long story short: my car is stuck near my dad's house. I don't know which way I was driving. I was . . . pursued. There's no sane way to explain it. Sorry, this is literally nuts. I swear I'm uh . . . I'm not crazy. My rental is stuck in mud. Oh. I'm within walking distance of Gunnar's Gas & Groceries. I might go there. It's not safe sitting in the car, so can you please, please, come get me? My phone is dying. Please help me, Rick. Please. Shit. I guess I made this into a long story after all—" The voicemail beeped.

Gina resumed her self-soothing ritual. "Iowa, Kansas, Kentucky, Michigan, Minnesota . . ." She slurped whatever dregs remained in the empty bottle. Inside her skin came the familiar whirring of a bender gaining momentum. The equivalent of the roller coaster notching up to its apex. Pretty soon, she'd be hunting for more booze. She eyed the other bottle. No. She'd made the deal. She couldn't break the deal. With herself, though? Who would find out?

*NO. NO. Gonna walk to the gas station, wait inside for Rick. Grab a coffee, and that's it.*

She opened the door and swung her legs out. "Mississippi, Missouri, Montana. . ." Confirmed no spider monsters poised to attack. Only prairie grass and red mud, now oozing into her boots. "Nebraska . . ."

But Gina missed a spot.

Her car was on a property with a lawn the length of a football field that ran up to a farmhouse, and behind the farmhouse, a turbulence had coalesced into a dark mass.

"Nevada, New Jersey, New Hampshire. . ." Gina took five squishy steps toward the road, her boots sinking a few inches into red mud. ". . . New Mexico, New York. Shit." Putrid fumes clotted the air.

*Gee-nuh.*

Her knees faltered, but she remained on her feet as she pivoted around as best she could in the sludge.

The storm rose above the pitched roof as if waiting for her to get far enough away from the vehicle before attacking. Its spider shape had transformed into something more akin to Mothra. Every flap of its "wings" fanned the choking death stench at her.

"Oh shit!"

Her boots made wet smacking sounds as she turned back to the car.

It was a race.

The mass billowed around the farmhouse, swooping down the lawn.

Every step Gina took sank her deeper. She howled in frustration, still eight feet from safety.

The mass ballooned to twice its size as it pressed forward.

Gina's left foot dropped into an old gopher hole up to her ankle. "Please, please!" She fell on her ass trying to pull it free. "Goddamnit!" The scent of chlorine stung her nose. Her hair stood on end.

"Oh no."

She heaved herself to a standing position. Coughed and choked in the noxious air as she slogged back to her car. *Left foot. . .right foot. Go, go, go . . .*

Lightning hacked the empty sky.

She wrenched open the door—

— and leapt inside —

— too late.

# A Trip Through Time & Bodies

WHEN
LIGHTNING
STRIKES CLOSE

When lightning strikes close do you have a fear of loss and calamity? There is never anything to be gained by a loss, but have a Hartford policy to take away that fear of calamity and complete loss. Hartford saves the farmer many a fear and worry. Always have a Hartford for complete protection.

WILSEY STATE BANK
F. I. Walker, Cashier.

# Chapter Twenty-Six

Floppy and amorphous, Gina became a jellyfish thrown into a frying pan, convulsing at the heat sizzling across her gelatinous skin.

Then fire turned to ice as she plummeted through a dark space emptied of everything but snippets of her past floating inside individual bubbles. *I'm dying and these are my last gifts*, she thought, reaching for a bubble containing her first kiss. It danced around her fingers and floated into the shadows.

Next came a bubble of the day her sixth-grade teacher Miss Grimm gave her an encouraging talk, emphasizing the importance of taking her drawings seriously. Oh, to have entered this memory to recapture the thrill of knowing she excelled at something and might have a purpose in life.

A twinkle drew her to the hike she and Mom took in the Burbank Hills when they saw a momma bear and its cub cross their trail not twenty feet away. A precious moment and salve, especially after Mom told her she was sick but Gina should stay strong because life was a beautiful confection no matter its ending. And then the recollection flickered off.

In fact, every positive memory eluded her, replaced by grimmer denizens in this odd jet stream.

A pink-frosted cake with candles pulled her back twenty-three years to her childhood kitchen. Gina observed this scene through the black button eyes of the Kitchen Witch hanging on the wall by the pantry.

Mom sang "Happy Birthday" to her Gina ballerina, who wore witch hats and glue mustaches, who frustrated teachers and unnerved her peers, who once pissed in the coat closet and licked Rick's cupcake like a porn star. Today she turned seven.

Also at the table sat Lexina, the new princess doll whose head Gina had turned so she and it wouldn't make eye contact. Gina didn't have the heart to tell her mom she hated dolls, so she humored her by doing what other little girls did and brought her along for the celebration.

She'd just blown out the candles when Dad breezed into the kitchen, tore off a hunk of cake, shoving it into his mouth with blood-crusted hands. Mom asked about the blood. Dad said he helped a friend kill a sow. "Soon, we'll be filthy rich in bacon!"

Young-Gina cried for the pig. Mom told Dad this was why she didn't invite Gina's friends over.

Dad kneeled before Young-Gina. He stunk bad as the garbage can. Said he was sorry he missed the party, such as it was. "The piggy's death was quick," he repeated as he hugged her tight.

Mom griped about the blood he got on Gina's birthday dress. The argument escalated into upended chairs and a smashed cake, into mutual slaps and Dad shaking Mom by the shoulders. Mom wrenched free and dragged her sticky, screaming daughter through the door leading down to the storm cellar.

Future-Gina detached from the Kitchen Witch to follow them.

In the dark stairwell. Locks flipped. A piece of wood propped against the door for fortification. Dad pounded on the other side as they descended into the cellar where sunshine strained through the dirty strips of windows beneath the ceiling.

Mom pulled a key and a padlock out of a metal box, then disappeared up the other stairs that led to the outside. Gina was on the verge of whimpering when Mom returned and told her she'd been locking the outside access doors. Also, "You're going to be okay, Gina. I saw into the future. I saw you as an adult, a beautiful woman."

*Whoa.* No memory of those words.

Mom told Gina to sit in Grandma's old rocking chair under the window. When tornadoes neared, everyone moved away from the window, but today's storm raged in the kitchen, so under the window was safer.

Footsteps stalked the floor above.

Mom stared at the ceiling, no expression on her face. Young-Gina decided Mom was like a doll, living in captivity on Daddy's shelf. This revelation made her feel grown up.

"Is he going to get in?"

"He'd better hope not." Mom touched the gun in her pocket she thought Gina couldn't see.

Future-Gina joined the dust mites swimming through shafts of sunlight, as if someone had shaken a snow globe.

*Clank-clank-clank.*

Dad, outside now, tried to muscle open the storm doors.

*Clank-clank-clank.*

Mom stood before Gina, arms around her as a human shield.

Dad screamed and screamed in a language she didn't understand.

Then he fell quiet. Mom and Gina strained to hear footfalls, words, creaks, anything. This was the first time Gina experienced raw terror.

Future-Gina relived the event with similar emotions, even knowing how it ended. In this quiet waiting, she startled when her shadow fell on Mom and Young-Gina. But it wasn't hers. It belonged to Dad, hunkered belly-down outside the window, hawking his family with bright blue eyes and a mouth twisted into a hungry smile, which remained on his face even as he slammed his forehead into the glass.

*BLAM-BLAM-BLAM.*

The glass cracked.

Mom pushed Gina over to the stairs. "Stay there!" She pulled the gun from her pocket, hand shaking so hard Gina feared it'd go off and shoot her.

Dad's boot smashed through the glass.

"Cover your ears, baby!"

Gina obeyed.

*BANG!*

Dad collapsed. Mom aimed again. Gina cried, "No!" so loud Mom dropped the gun.

Both parents wept. Dad's eyes transformed back to their normal browns.

"I'm sorry I ruined your birthday. I'm a rotten pile of shit. Kill me! Please kill me!"

The bullet had grazed his calf. Forehead lacerations from the broken glass didn't require stitches. Mom cleaned and bandaged him. Then he disappeared into the barn.

That night, Mom crowded into Gina's bed after placing a chair under the doorknob. She talked about California and the ocean and going to see Jimmy Kimmel.

Later, Dad rapped on the door. What Momma called a "polite knock."

"You sleeping in there tonight?" His voice was drunk-thick.

"Yes."

The following day they'd sneak out through the cellar and drive non-stop to the West Coast. Gina tossed Lexina out the window somewhere near the Grand Canyon.

Mom, a few years older than Gina was now, cradled her child as they stared at the moon. Future-Gina tried to curl in bed beside them when a force yanked her from the room.

## Chapter Twenty-Seven

Damp, dusty, cold. Pearly winter light outside the window. Gina stood within the barn, bearing witness through someone else's eyes, a view akin to watching a stage show. Curtains rose, revealing the provocative tableau of a man crumpled into an old claw-foot bathtub.

The jockey-sized fellow with a hatchet lodged dead-center in his face, eyes open and lolling to either side, looked to be in his sixties, or road-filthy forties. The mystery of his disappearance would never be solved.

Blue light flickered around the edges of the scene.

*"Nemo te requiret, spurcissime drifter."* Dad's voice. Gina understood it to mean, "No one will miss you, filthy drifter."

A work boot pushed against the man's chest. Hands clutched the ax shaft and withdrew the blade, raking up gore and bone. As a finale, the bifurcated head folded in on itself with the squelch of a collapsing sinkhole.

Pleasure radiated through her body. An ovation. Primal but not sexual. A beast of prey enjoying its power.

"*Adolebitque in flamma.*" (Burn in my flame.)
By the time the flame materialized, Gina was elsewhere.

# Chapter Twenty-Eight

Afternoon in the backyard of the farmhouse, where young and beautiful Mom, in the colorful senorita dress she wore when summers got steamy, hung clothes on the line.

# Chapter Twenty-Nine

One night in her darkened bedroom, Young-Gina peered through the spider's eye tasked with observing the barn as Dad's truck coasted up the driveway with headlights off. The truck turned around and backed up to the barn doors. Brake lights cast a red glow against them, providing enough visibility for Gina to notice a tarp over the truck bed. When the brake lights blinked off, Gina squinted in the dark until her eyes adjusted.

Dad opened the truck's gate, untied the tarp, and balled it up. Underneath was a bicycle, and another tarp, this one cigar-shaped. Dad pulled out the bike and leaned it against the side of the barn. Then he tugged the cigar-shaped tarp across the truck bed. The end of it fell off the gate, and an arm came dangling out, fingers brushing the dirt.

# Chapter Thirty

Full moon on the midnight highway. She was driving a small pickup truck. The hands on the steering wheel belonged to Dad. Too afraid to peer into the rearview mirror, she focused on the road ahead, empty except for a pair of red taillights in the distance. Intoxicated by expectation—of something yet unknown—she turned off her own headlights and reduced speed.

Those taillights swerved, veered across the oncoming lane, and swung up, pointing to the sky. Dust rose. A horn droned.

As the pickup tracked closer to its prey, Gina experienced the same delirium as when alcohol overcame worries and made her feel invincible. Any hyperactivity inside her head manifested as an almost sensual delight at seeing the disabled car, a green Volvo with a surfboard on its roof and nose-first in a deep swale. Her vehicle stopped three car lengths behind.

Boots clomped down the road, kicking aside pieces of tire. Dad's hand picked up a spike strip and returned to the pickup. A *clunk* as the strip landed in the truck bed. Then back to the Volvo. Breath clouds in the night cold. The horn petered out. A flashlight *clicked* on, illuminating the longboard on the roof—the longboard stored in the barn.

She trudged through the muddy ditch to the driver's side door. Dad's reflection in the window. He wore a large bandage on his forehead.

Inside, an unconscious young man with his head on the steering wheel. Shaggy brown hair. Puka shell bracelet.

Excitement thrummed down into her abdomen. The door opened. So did Dad's mouth. As the flame began its journey, Gina clamped her eyes shut, unwilling to see what happened next.

## Chapter Thirty-One

Mom, wearing a bathrobe in the kitchen of the place she now lived, stared blankly at the coffee maker because she'd forgotten how it worked.

*Goddamnit.*

## Chapter Thirty-Two

Fog gathered on the outskirts of a gas station on a rural highway. Gina sat in the driver's seat of a pickup truck. In the rearview mirror, she met her father's eyes, shimmering a supernatural sky blue with tiny lightning bolts winking inside his gigantic black pupils. Behind them lurked whatever drove his body.

Their gaze penetrated the gloom of a developing storm to fix on a young woman at the pump filling a gas can. Late teens. Cornsilk hair. Petite. Slim. Tight jeans. Heart-shaped rump. No car in sight.

A roll of thunder hastened the girl's work. She capped the can and hurried to the road.

Truck headlights clicked on. Dim yellow orbs bathed the world in sepia. Once the girl got to the road, the truck crept forward. Its engine made predator growls, elated by the hunt.

Between the windshield wipers, she sloshed through mud puddles. Her long blonde hair flattened in the rain.

Feeling his eyes on her, the girl turned, squinted at the headlights. She reeked of vulnerability. Was it the crowded buck teeth, perhaps? Or the full lips gathered around the teeth? Maybe she was a truck stop hooker, or someone's runaway daughter, or a girl who needed braces. Gina wasn't sure if these musings belonged to her or to Dad.

The girl stood her ground as the truck drew closer. Despite the rain, she held her chin high with the false bravado of a woman alone in the night. Gina wanted to scream, "Smash the can into his face!" or, "Run into the fields!" But all she could do was stare at the Christian fish medallion the girl wore on a chain resting in the valley between her breasts.

Excitement built in the groin area—sickening and out-of-her-control thrilling. Whatever happened next, she wouldn't be able to blink away or hurl herself into the slip-stream and hope to wake up to a better nightmare.

The window lowered, spilling a Keith Urban ballad into the night.

"Need a lift?" Her father's voice sounded so young and earnest.

The girl offered him a shy, toothy smile as she stepped closer. "Praise God." A sweet, breathy voice. "It's so nice to find a good Samaritan. Me and my little brother—"

Fast as a snake's tongue, Dad used both hands to snag the necklace and her hair. In the scuffle, the medallion broke off and fell into the mud.

The girl's choking protestations diminished under an insistent *beep-beep-beep* . . .

# Infiltration

## Lightning Does Repeat

OBSERVATIONS of the United States Forest Service question the truth of the old saying that "Lightning never strikes twice in the same place." In certain zones, the forest experts say, lightning may be counted on with every electrical storm and with the accumulating of data the experts hope to map out the zones where lightning strikes most frequently and thus to install more effective fire guards. More than half of the 6,078 forest fires in National forests in 1920 were set by lightning.

# Chapter Thirty-Three

Lights throbbed in and out of focus, keeping time with a beeping sound. Gina tried but couldn't raise her head, thanks to the thousands of shooting stars gestating inside her left arm and shooting up into her neck. The moment she imagined how the stars might look if she could see through her skin, they exploded across her skin. Every inch of her itched, then tickled, then ached. She'd scratch the stars away if only her arm would move.

Time passed, and the pain dulled until she'd swear she was floating in a swimming pool, holding the edge of a raft while her legs drifted free and her body roiled in a sustained aftershock.

A rust-hewed halo moved into the light. "Hello," said a male voice smelling of cigarettes under a breath mint.

"I know you," Gina said, forgetting his name.

Rusty Halo leaned in closer. "I'm glad you're okay, Gina. "

Her name on his lips produced lovely echoes. "Gina . . .Gina . . ."

In a languorous blink of the eye, a silver halo floating above a white coat replaced Rusty Halo.

"Are you the doctor?" Gina's voice came out weak and soupy.

She, an older lady, offered a beatific smile. "I am, yes. You can call me Virginia. I believe Gina is a diminutive of Virginia. Is that your full name? Virginia? Like mine?"

"No. Just Gina."

"Gina." She ran a pen around her clipboard. "Are you aware of what happened to you?"

Gina tried to nod.

Virginia pulled a tissue from her pocket, folded it into a small rectangle, and dabbed the drool gathered in the corners of Gina's mouth. As Gina's vision sharpened, she noticed the doctor wore a small gold cross, had skin smooth as a vintage handbag, thick white hair, and friendly eye wrinkles. Something strange about the eyes, though. Time-share salesperson's eyes.

"Tell me how bad, doctor."

Virginia balled up the drool tissue and tucked it into her pocket.

"The electrocution caused light burns on your back and more significant burns on the index and middle fingers of your left hand where the current entered. We drained the blisters and treated the fingertips with antibiotics. They're wrapped in a light gauze with medical tape. One of your ribs has a minor fracture, so we recommend taking deep breaths as often as possible."

"How did I get here?"

Rusty Halo poked his head in to say, "You called me from the car."

Rick! Rusty-Halo-Rick!

"I don't remember. Hi, Rick." Gina reached for him, but her arm still wouldn't budge.

"There's an exit wound up by your clavicle," Virginia continued. "Your hair on that side is . . . the EKG shows your heart is fine. A very lucky girl you are."

"Did you carry me to your car, Rick?" Gina's glassy eyes slow-danced across Rick's unshaven chin. "Carry me through the mud, Rick?"

"Enough of this." Virginia shooed him away with a flick of her wrist.

*Not fair!*

The pattering of multiple soft-soled shoes told of other people leaving the room.

Virginia pressed a button on the metal side rail, raising Gina a bit, then held up a glass of water with a bendy straw aimed at her lips. Gina took a sip.

"Do you have a relationship with Christ?" Virginia asked.

High or not, Gina regarded the question as inappropriate and pushed away the straw with her tongue. "Huh?"

"Are you a Christian?"

Gina caught a glimpse of herself reflected in Virginia's glasses, with a fan of black hair against the white pillow—on only one side of her head!

"Oh shit, did half my hair burn off?"

Virginia nodded yes.

"Is my scalp burned?"

"No worse than a bad sunburn."

Again, she offered Gina the straw. Gina shook her head.

"I'll have someone check on you soon, Miss Fade."

"Nonne aliquis vocare matrem meam?" Gina asked.

Virginia did a double-take. "Pardon? Can you say that

in English? Or slower? My Latin is rusty. You said something about your Mom?"

"Did anybody call my mom?" Somehow Gina spoke Latin. *Huh.*

"I'm not sure. Let me . . ." She backed away with whispery steps until she was out of Gina's eyeline.

"Hello?" Gina raised her head off the pillow high enough to understand she was alone in the room. Ceiling lights drew further away, as if looking through the wrong end of binoculars. A force inside her separated and prodded, testing the confines of its cage.

*That's not good.*

Gina conked out again.

# Chapter Thirty-Four

Dreams assault, push, cajole, rend. They'll paralyze you from jarring yourself awake and confound you into believing they're real. Gina sank into their depths, drilling through a stratum of progressively bleaker feelings as millions of years passed. Hunger provided impetus for her drive, for her rage, for her insatiable need to eat. But *what* to eat?

She soared over a sea spanning the Gulf of Mexico to the Arctic, and from the Rockies to the Appalachians. The sea swarmed with giant apex predators like the undulating Mosasaur with its double-hinged jaw, while Pteranodons filled the sky. Still, these eons brought her scarce bounty. The glory was in the spitting and howling, in stalking a Pteranodon who got too close to the clouds. Otherwise, not much else to burn.

Ice came. Ice melted. Its water funneled into rivers and streams, bringing forth trees and grass and mammals. When the bipeds arrived, the burning unleashed mass terror. To track a biped on the plains brought frissons of pure pleasure. The release was in the dragon's kiss.

Her master, the biggest, oldest, and most powerful inter-dimensional beast controlling the portals, had determined the territory and boundaries, which was an enormous chunk of what became central Kansas—from the flatlands to the hills—eighty-five million years later.

She butchered trees. Left her imprints in the dirt. Blackened rocks. Frightened farmers. Happiness sounded delicious. As did love, hope, contentment. All she needed to do was take it from someone. Take it, eat it, expel it, then eat it again and again until its satiety dimmed, compelling her to stalk fresher harvest. In these dreams, she gorged, yet remained hungry, wretched, and lonely. She despised herself. She despised the world. None of it could fill her.

In the now times, she swirled around the Flint Hills. Feverish and aflame. Forked tongues snapped at outcrops of flinty limestone bedrock and scorched tallgrass. She cloaked herself in electrostatic discharges and defied all laws of meteorological science by separating from the chain to cast her gaze across the flatlands at the church with the arched window, and at the man inside, laid out on a table.

*George.*

## Chapter Thirty-Five

Gina woke up ready to assess her reality in the calm, objective way she'd learned through years of emerging from alcoholic blackouts.

Inset ceiling lights. The kind they put in fancy kitchens. A long, slim window high on the wall. Light peeking around the drawn shades. Walls unadorned except for a framed print of a lion with a halo. Must be a religious hospital. Halos. A memory of halos—rusty, silver. When did the halos visit her? How long ago?

No TV. She pushed the button on the bed rail, and a gentle hum sounded as the bed folded into a seated position. Top-notch equipment. Speaking of which, the vitals monitor was gone.

To her left, a side table containing a plastic daisy in a vase and a devotional booklet with Jesus on the cover. No phone or call button.

Self-assessment: a square of gauze secured by Band-Aids on her left hand where the IV had been. Bandaging on the two fingers. More bandaging below her clavicle, stretching over her shoulder blade, and across to her back.

She stared at the blankets over her legs, steeling herself for the worst, then yanked them off. Everything appeared normal. Relieved, she lowered the bed rail and swung her legs free. Booties touched down on a laminate wood floor. With her right hand on the mattress, she crab-walked to the foot of the bed.

The door to her room stood ajar.

A splotch of red brought her eyes to the red and black plaid connected to jeans and boots on the bottom and a corpulent neck and sandy hair on top. A dude napped on a chair outside her door. Legs splayed, hands folded across his stomach. He must be dozing.

This wasn't Rick. Might be the big guy whose paws she slapped away at the funeral. Why was the church here?

*Uram te ab intus, bitch,* (I will burn you from the inside, bitch), whispered the inner voice. Again, she understood the Latin, and as baffling as that was, her first order of business must be locating her phone and her stuff. She lifted her hands from the mattress, found equilibrium, and set out for the two long, slender cabinets against the wall.

Nothing in the first cabinet. The other cabinet held her boots, jeans, and sweater. Dizziness threatened as she bent over to fetch them. She held the cabinet door for fear of fainting, breathing deep and slow until her head cleared.

She shuffled over to the bed to put on her sweater and jeans. To her relief, she found the envelope with Lamb money still in her pocket. Now, phone. Back to the cabinet. On the top shelf, she located a plastic bag containing her purse and phone. 13% battery left. Not good, but good enough.

Phone in hand, she squeezed herself into the long cabinet as best she could for a tall girl and shut the door as far as it would go. She called Mom and got her voicemail.

Gina spoke in a hush. "I'm in a hospital in Kansas. I was struck by lightning. Not joking. I'm alive, obviously. Call me back. I have to get out of here. Shit. I don't know if you even check voicemail anymore. Anyway, call me. If my phone dies, I'm in the hospital in . . . Ellsworth? Get a pen and paper. Where am I? I'm gonna find out. Hold on."

She backed out of the cabinet, eyes seeking a medical chart or anything that would identify the hospital. If a guy weren't sleeping outside her door, she'd go find a nurse and ask. "Mom. I don't know the name. Call hospitals in the Ellsworth area. Ellsworth, Kansas. Write it down. Write down 'Ellsworth Hospital, Gina Fade, electrocution.' I mean I doubt there's a rash of electrocutions—" The voicemail ended with a loud *BEEP*.

Damn. Was it loud enough to rouse her guard?

She peeked through the gap between the door and the cabinet and was relieved to see his boots hadn't moved.

Who else to call? Rick. Voicemail again. She hung up and texted, "COME GET ME." Rusty Halo knew where she was.

12% on the phone.

Amy. Damn. She'd never called Amy on this phone. Where was Dad's phone? Purse. Purse. Okay. Back to the bed, to her purse, where she'd tossed Dad's phone, then, what she vowed would be her last trip into the cabinet. She closed its door and redialed the last number to call her.

"Hello?" That inimitable voice of a knife scraping burnt toast almost brought her to tears.

"Thank God. I'm in the hospital. I got struck by lightning—"

"Oh, dear Mary."

"I'm fine. I guess. Please come pick me up. You can take me to your church, I don't care—"

"Are you hearing a voice?"

Sharp fingers poked the back side of Gina's eyeballs.

"What if I said yes?"

Amy panted. Must be weighing options. Amy would taste gritty and brittle. Also, the way she clung to life even in the towering shadow of death would add a sweetness to her destruction.

"Are you still there? Is this what happened to Dad? How did he get rid of it?" In her growing desperation, Gina had notched up the volume, caught herself, and whispered, "I mean, he must have, right?"

"Faith healing worked once. Didn't stick, what with the empty prayers of hypocrites." Amy made a dismissive noise that turned into a cough.

"You're sure it's safe at your house?"

"Yes. In the east, it doesn't go past the Smoky Hills. In the west, it's stuck on this side of Sunflower Peak."

"Okay, I'm ready. Come get me."

"When I arrive, you will not make eye contact. You keep your eyes on the car or the ground. And stay in the backseat. I'll drive you straight to Father Doyle."

"Please hurry."

"What hospital are you in?"

"I don't know. There's no signage, or chart, or nurse button."

"Oh, dear. Mother Mary, help you—"

"What? Why? Why?"

"You all right, Miss Fade?" asked the deep male voice behind her.

# Chapter Thirty-Six

Gina dropped the phone. "Shit!"

A tomato-faced vision of malevolence hulked in the open doorway.

"You should rest, Gina."

He, one of the henchmen from the church, tilted his head, flicking long, sandy-hewed, side-parted bangs off a freckled forehead.

"Hi. Thanks for your concern, but I'm good." She scooped the phone off the floor, frowning at the lost call. "I need to find a charger. My mom and grandmother are concerned—"

"Doctor said you shouldn't get all stirred up." His didn't look up from the cell in his enormous paw.

"How am I stirred up?"

He shrugged. "You were the one yelling inside the closet."

"Could you give me a little privacy so I can find my charger?"

He jabbed his index finger around on his phone, messaging someone.

"Okay, is that a no?"

Reaching behind him, he pulled the door closed. "You wait for the doctor." He flicked his bangs again. "I'll plug the phone in for you." He made grabby hands for her cell, but Gina snapped it back, hugging it to her chest.

"I'm not going to hurt you, Gina."

"The only people who say that are the people who are going to hurt someone, bro."

"You should calm down."

"I don't know you. I'm not a member of your church, so why're you outside my door?"

He took two flat-footed steps closer. "Come on, Miss Fade, give it over, and I'll go plug it in for you."

As he spoke, monotone and threatening, something inside her gathered cyclonic momentum and rose into her esophagus.

"We're here to help you, Gina."

"We?"

"The church."

"The church can suck my forty-foot dick!" The words emerged deeper and louder than she expected. The big man's mouth dropped into a startled O. "I'll burn all you fuckin' Lambs and eat you in a curry!"

The second outburst knocked him onto the bed, and her against the cabinets.

In contrast to his potato body, the man sprang to his feet. He pulled a necklace out of his flannel shirt. At the end of its chain dangled a three-inch wooden cross.

Gina circled him, delighting in his timid retreat to the far side of the bed, hand quaking as he brandished his talisman.

"*Minima, territus animal!*" (Tiny, frightened animal!)

she/it said, experiencing visions of his skin blackening like a campfire marshmallow.

"I rebuke you!"

"Ain't that cute?" Gina sidled up to him as he pressed himself further into the corner.

"In the name of Jesus . . ." He slid down the wall to a seated position, squishing his eyes shut when Gina leaned into him. She tore the cross from the chain and pitched it across the room.

"It's loose! It's loose!" the man screamed.

Gina's bravado dissipated and she fled, confused about what was loose. The cross? Herself? She slammed the door behind her. Locked it—perplexed that it had a lock—and stood there catching her breath.

*What the hell just happened?*

Frantic pounding on the other side fired her jets. She flew down the hallway, eyes peeled for medical staff or exit signs. The empty corridor made no sense, nor did all the high windows.

*Oh God.* Gina suddenly grasped what Amy had tried to tell her. She wasn't sprinting down a hospital corridor; she was in the church's basement.

Behind her, a great crunching noise. He'd kicked the door off its hinges, and now his boots thundered in hot pursuit.

Gina turned the only corner, spotted the exit sign over a door. She bumped the door open with her hip and entered a stairwell painted aqua blue. Everything about the so-called exit put ice in her veins, especially the door at the top of the stairs, which she expected to either melt away or explode.

Escape couldn't be this easy.

Still, she scrambled up the stairs, getting halfway when the door opened. At the top of the stairs stood a woman in scrubs, her hair piled high and long pink nails catching the light. Tawny, the pastor's wife.

"There you are, you little dickens." Her open-toed pumps clacked on the metal stairs as she descended. "Will you please stop making problems for us?"

Behind Gina, the door burst open. Hot breath curdled the back of her neck. "Give me the phone." The henchman's freckled paw vice-gripped her wrist until she dropped it. Then he grabbed her other arm as well, holding her still as Tawny plunged a needle into her neck.

Gina gawped at the lunatic images of an empty syringe held between long, pink sabers, and the matching pink lips curled back from the teeth. The eyes weren't as fierce. They seemed wary.

*Of me.*

In seconds, the dim yellow safety lights, the blue metal stairs, and the pink lips disappeared as Gina's world irised shut.

She landed on a conveyor belt and couldn't move. A warbling soundtrack of calliopes, hell screams, and lightning strikes accompanied her journey to the main event: the stitched-up mouth of her father's corpse.

When she got within spitting distance, his mouth wheezed open. The mortician's stitches tore through rotten flesh. White goo oozed from the gashes.

"Gee-nuh! Gina ballerina!" His voice, a dead voice, called to her repeatedly.

Mangled lip giblets tickled her like car wash brushes as she passed under Dad's teeth and into the mouth.

# POP!

It Pays to Be Safe
Don't wait until it is too late. Remember Lightning strikes and destroys millions of dollars worth of property and kills hundreds of people every year.
You have no assurance that this season it may not be your turn to be struck—unless you get Shinn-Flat protection now.
Protect Now—Before Lightning Strikes!
Shinn-Flat
Prevents Lightning Losses
Shinn-Flat is superior to any other form of rod or conductor, for these reasons:
1—It is woven in a flat cable, with greater carrying capacity for electricity.
4—The Shinn patented four-legged Brace, with self-locking feature, holds top always in place.
5—Shinn-Flat is always installed by our licensed Dealer, whom we have instructed.
6—A cash Bond issued by a large Bonding Company insures your money back if damage by Lightning occurs.
Lightning Can't Strike
Shinn Gets There First
Esbon Hardware Co.

# Chapter Thirty-Seven

"What is your name?"

The pastor stood dangerously close to Gina's body. Beneath his shiny suit dwelled a prime cut of meat marbled with fat for added flavor. She'd be delighted to gnaw through the porous epidermis, a delicious sugar-spun shell protecting the tender juices inside.

"Tell me your name!"

"Perditor! (*Destroyer!*)"

"Where is my sister?"

"*Caro sororis tuae dulce et crispum gustavit.*" (The flesh of your sister tasted sweet and crispy.)

"In the name of Jesus Christ, tell me!"

A stinging slap brought Gina to the surface, stunned and irritated.

"Ow! Asshole! What are you doing?" She tried to throw a punch, but someone had tied her arms to a padded surface. Same with her legs and torso.

Familiar long pink fingernails entered from above and pushed her head back down.

"Where is my sister?" The pastor loomed over her, his slapping hand still cocked.

"I don't know what you're talking about!"

Tawny clamped a hand over Gina's mouth as the pastor retreated to the cabal of Sandies hovering around an enormous desk.

Gina's eyes roamed the vaulted ceiling, painted the same sky blue as the exit stairwell. *Oh, sweet exit.* Bleached wood beams crisscrossed under the peaked ceiling. Over by the arched window, a big, fancy Bible stood on a pedestal.

An energy built itself inside her eardrums, buzzing as it grew. Gina shook her head, yawned as if it were a bad case of air pressure, but it only grew louder and somehow bigger until the sound of a *Pop* sent her body shooting up to the ceiling. She raised her arms to cushion a collision with the beams but soared straight through them and circled around to hover.

Below, five men were still in deep conversation with their backs turned on Gina, who lay strapped to a gurney by her hands and feet. Tawny took her hand off Gina's mouth so she could bite at a hangnail.

*Am I dead? Am I a ghost?*

Gina-on-the-gurney opened her eyes. Brown irises turned to a piercing blue as she smiled up at Gina, who floated.

*I win.*

Once upon a time, Gina scarfed a handful of shrooms and got onto a human slingshot ride at a carnival—terrified, elated, airborne, and screaming. She had the identical feeling now as another *Pop* sent her essence screeching through time and reality back to Dad's kitchen.

# Chapter Thirty-Eight

A wood-burning stove and the absence of a refrigerator meant that she'd gone back in time. An old woman stood at the back door, looking out its window at the yard.

Gina had only to wonder what the woman saw before she found herself outside, between the clothesline and the apricot tree, where a man dug a small hole with a large shovel. Resting by his feet was a potato sack cinched with twine. He took a break to wipe sweat from his brow with a red bandana. His eyes blazed blue.

George the First! A revelation so alarming she gasped, to which George dropped the shovel and leaped back from the hole, eyes cartwheeling around in search of the source.

*Pop!*

# Chapter Thirty-Nine

In a hospital room without a phone or television, a different old woman sat in bed with perfect posture as a nurse gave her a sponge bath. Was this the "Poor Gina" Amy mentioned? Luigiana? Whose possession they mistook for what is now known as dementia? The nurse hummed as she ran a sponge down the elderly woman's arm.

Luigiana's eyes found Gina and turned blue, though a bit more cornflower than the others' aquas. The nurse glided the sponge back up her arm with gentle, circular motions. When she got to the shoulder, Luigiana seized her arm and took a bite out of it. Flames flitted around her lips.

*Pop!*

# Chapter Forty

This trip brought her living room back to the era when the original television still worked. Dad, around eight years old, nosed through the curtains to keep watch on the barn. He spoke to her in his adult voice, "You shouldn't have come to Kansas, Gina Ballerina."

*Pop!*

# Chapter Forty-One

Upon re-entry to her body on the gurney, Gina got another slap across the face from the pastor.

"Stop hitting me!"

"Tell me your name!"

"I'm Gina. Fade."

"See? She's fine, Ed. It's her." A familiar voice.

"Open your eyes and your ears, brother. She's lying to us!" The pastor's voice cracked as if he might cry or scream.

"What happened to the plan about praying?" Rick's voice! Rick would help her! "You said we'd all get together and pray this thing out, so why aren't we praying?"

"Realistically, on a scale of zero to ten, guess the success rate of casting a demon from a non-believer?"

"Didn't you help her father?"

"Yes, but he believed, and it never stopped searching for him. What if it sees one of us? Do you want to be hunted?"

"No, pastor. But isn't everything possible with faith?"

"The answer to *my* question is zero. The chances of casting a demon from a non-believer. A zero percent success rate. And only Jesus walked on the water."

"So did Peter!"

"That's one guy."

"Please don't do this!"

*Do what?* Gina and her occupier wondered.

*Pop!*

# Chapter Forty-Two

She could've been riding a witch's broom the way she swept across the porch and nearly collided with herself. Gina-on-the-porch didn't notice, being too dreamy-eyed as she watched Rick drive away. Future-Gina had seen that face in the mirror many times; the face of intoxication and need.

What a pisser. The church had deployed him to meat-hook her. A real honey, that Rick. Handsome, adorably shy, an aw-shucks guy with a firm ass, soulful eye contact, and a history with the heathen progeny of George Fade III. Her befuddled state made her the perfect sucker.

*Pop!*

# Chapter Forty-Three

Wind thwacked the window. Wind chimes brayed on the porch, and yet Gina heard only the wet, sloppy chewing in the kitchen, where Past-Gina stuffed giant forkfuls of cheesy tots into her mouth.

Future-Gina observed from within the Kitchen Witch until her essence or spirit or ghost or whatever grew too big for the doll to contain and breached the fabric, flapping her wings as she transformed into the black-cloud Mothra, desperate to warn herself to abandon the tater tots and get the fuck out.

This Gina permutation possessed a single power: occupying time for longer periods. In her new reality, she moved at normal speed, while the world traveled past in slow motion.

Past-Gina spotted her as a reflection in the window, but by the time she screamed and turned, Gina-Kitchen-Witch had already sailed out the door, and when she blew outside, she became the storm.

*Pop!*

# Chapter Forty-Four

Future-Gina experienced a montage of the various moments in which she blew on Past-Gina's neck or back, trying so hard to get her to leave. The blowing was actually a series of shrieked admonitions lost in the chaos of a time differential.

# Chapter Forty-Five

Gina's different frame rate allowed her time to straight-arm TV Guides off the shelves, then arrange them into a funeral pyre, ready for burning. As a huge horror movie fan, Gina scared easily. Future-Gina counted on that. If she succeeded, Past-Gina would skip meeting with Amy and drive straight to the airport. Why wouldn't she after this? Come on! Turned out she didn't, but that was in the past. Now, right now, was also the past *and* the present, and it was all so fucking confusing.

Future-Gina relived the full-body tension as she watched herself enter the parlor and sidle up to the shelf. She tried to push Past-Gina but couldn't. How was she able to touch the books but not herself? A fond memory surfaced when Gina recognized *Oh, the Places You'll Go!* Future-Gina held the book in place, waiting until Past-Gina reached for it, then hurled it to the floor. She really spooked it up by fanning the pages to the beginning and the end. Her time clocked in at a leisurely sixty seconds, while in Corporeal-Gina's time, it happened in six.

*Today is your day! Your mountain is waiting. So . . . Get on your way!*

*Pop!*

## Chapter Forty-Six

When Gina came back for the papers—when it caught her—Future-Gina raced her to the front door and pushed it closed. She didn't even need to touch it! So amazed by her newfound telekinesis, she hesitated, allowing Past-Gina to outwit her and exit through the kitchen.

*Pop!*

# Chapter Forty-Seven

Gina wild-eyed the group of Lambs gaping down at her.

"What the hell is going on?"

Pastor Ed leaned in close. "Gina? Gina? Welcome back." The dulcet tones had returned to his voice, and he kept his hands clasped together in a prayer formation. "We were worried about you, young lady."

The idea of dying alone in a church in Kansas after working so hard to maintain sobriety and withstanding the crate full of Dad's liquor, but then fucking up in the car, filled her with such self-pity she blubbered like someone on dental meds.

"Three days ago, I was on the Harbor Freeway going downtown, and I didn't get off the exit for Uncle Joe's liquor, and I was proud of myself, so I called my dad. I fucking killed him. If I hadn't called . . ." The sobs took over, sobs matching in volume the steady hiss in her head. Gas turned on, awaiting the flame.

The pastor made soothing clucking sounds until the

sobbing stopped, then asked, "Who is inside you and where is my sister?"

She raised her head to look for Rick so she could tell him she might have fallen for him if he wasn't such a huge, betraying prick.

Pastor Ed took a firm hold of her chin. "Answer my questions."

"I'm pressing charges for assault!" The words dripped out slow and soupy.

Her eyes slid over to the Christian fish charm dangling from the pastor's tie. The charm disgorged an image of itself: in a mud puddle on the side of the highway.

*Pop!*

# Chapter Forty-Eight

Back in the pickup, parked somewhere off the road in a field. This time, Gina occupied the passenger seat. Rain clobbered its roof. Excited breaths fogged the windows. On the radio, a classic country dude sang about coming home at suppertime.

Gina surveyed her soggy jeans and muddy toes in sandals. The splayed legs implied unconsciousness, or worse. She was inside the girl. She felt nothing.

Seated to her left, young Dad rocked back and forth, occasionally banging his forehead on the wheel.

"It wasn't me, Gina Ballerina. It wasn't me!"

"How do I beat it, Dad?"

*Pop!*

# Chapter Forty-Nine

She stood next to Dad on the roof of his house. He balanced close to the edge, sobbing.

"Please, Dad, tell me what to do."

His head swiveled to her. Confusion in his astonishing blue eyes, then recognition.

"Gina Ballerina."

"What do I do?"

"One for many," he said, lifting his foot as if readying to step off.

Unseen bystanders screamed. A lightning bolt launched from his mouth and hit the barn. The force knocked him back, inches from the roof's edge. Flames flared across the barn's roof.

*Pop!*

# One for Many

The Coffeyville *Journal* of the 11th contains an account of the killing of Martin Phillips, a few miles west of that place, on the 9th, by lightning. Death was instantaneous. His age was 22 years. The sad event was rendered doubly tragical from the fact that only forty-six days before, a brother of the unfortunate man was also suddenly killed in the same way (by lightning), in the same neighborhood.

# Chapter Fifty

Nosediving back into her body was so intense that Gina's body lurched, unnerving the pastor's wife, who clutched her heart and squealed.

"Stop that!"

She glared at Gina for a moment before resuming her task of pushing the gurney down a corridor lined with lion and lamb paintings and LED wall sconces. Lights from the chapel glowed at the hallway's end.

"I am going to eat your hair and your skin," it said, using Gina's mouth.

The gurney stopped.

"Ed? Ed! It's talking to me!" Tawny's voice floated down the hallway. No response. "All right, hon. Lemme show you how we keep the dark things quiet." In seconds, she brandished her syringe.

Gina felt the prick on her shoulder and then the rush of benzo filling her. Given to a person without a history of massive drug tolerance, this might have put them out, but Gina faked the level of her high and let her eyelids fall.

Another set of footsteps approached. Gina kept her eyes closed, listening.

"Sorry, what happened?" Pastor Ed. Fancy-man cologne, breath spray. Did he drink in secret? Drinkers mask their sins with perfumes. She used cinnamon Altoids and hand sanitizer.

"It threatened me."

"She's tied down, darling. She can't hurt you. She's helpless." Pastor Ed's voice carried a note of regret.

"What's wrong, Ed? What's your face doing?"

Jagged panting in Gina's head blotted out much of their conversation.

*Be quiet so I can listen.*

*Fuck you.*

*We're both fucked if you don't shut up.*

The panting abated enough for Gina to hear Tawney tell him, "George said she'd been to a half-dozen rehabs, and none of them took."

"When did Christ ever turn away the afflicted?"

"This is beyond afflicted."

"But am I acting from a place of love?"

"Yeah, for the innocent people who aren't possessed."

"Her mother—she counts on her."

"George left money to take care of her mother."

*Mom?* Inside her, the beast guffawed. It thought it knew something Gina didn't.

*Listen!*

"And where *is* your sister, anyway? It won't tell you!" Tawny's voice grew more strident. "She's dust in the field or the wind or nowhere after all these years. She could've given you nephews and nieces! But she didn't, and you know why."

"Vengeance plays no part in this."

"Okay, then what if it comes after me? Or the kids? Will you be there to protect them when they go outside to play? What if a storm sneaks up like a snake in the grass? What if you and me don't see it until it's too late?"

"I wish the Lord would give me a sign." He let out a short, clipped sob.

"Don't, Ed. You want a sign? All you need do is look at the faces of your children, and that'll be your sign. And don't you think for a second this whole song and dance you did was anything but a way to get me to say 'Amen' to something you'd already set your mind to. I know how you play me." The gurney stopped. The couple groped and sniffed and kissed and made disgusting baby talk.

Gina risked a peek through her lashes. Doctor Virginia emerged from the beaming lights of the chapel as an elongated shadow and then resolved into an innocuous-looking spinster with a doctor's bag, which she placed on Gina's belly.

It would be so lovely to charbroil her white, leathery skin. And easy. But Gina held back. Unleashing something over which she had zero control was probably a shitty idea.

Doctor Virginia swiped a hand wipe across Gina's forehead, then patted it dry with a precisely folded tissue. She brought out a small jar with a lid so tight she had to hand it over to the pastor for help. "Thank you, Pastor."

She dipped her middle finger inside.

Gina moaned. She was getting her very own ash cross.

*I will make her into ashes.*

While Virginia drew the cross on Gina's forehead, she stared into Gina's eyes as though looking at a small bird on a faraway horizon.

The pastor released a mournful sigh. Tawny rubbed his back. "She's a vessel of evil, Ed. You're doing what's right."

"Thank you, darlin'. Thank you, Lord. I praise You and lift You high."

The gurney glided into the chapel.

## Chapter Fifty-One

Bright as an operating room, the chapel appeared ready for a ceremony, complete with witnesses milling about the altar in Dockers and button-down short-sleeve shirts and choral music playing soft enough so as not to sound like the soundtrack for a sacrifice.

*Sacrifice. Shit.*

Gina's lips had grown numb. The hissing inside her head vanished. This should have brought comfort. Nah. She and her occupier were both aware of how fucked she was.

*Maybe it's best to die.* The voice was Gina's, ready to give up, acquiescing to the idea of dying the way she'd spent much of the last decade—numb, detached, distracted, hopeless.

*No, no, no, I ride you first before you die, you wretched bitch.*

Over the last decade, Gina had escaped various unpleasant scenes intact, such as Squidgie's sex pantry, or naked unconsciousness at Burning Man, or waking up in a bus in a strange city and figuring out how to get home.

Could she do so again? Or had she reached the culmination of a misspent life, here in a cartoonishly bananas church, with her body occupied by some ancient demon?

*No,* she thought. She had goals. Rebuild her business, live untouched by addiction, have a future. How did a bunch of dimwit assholes get her to this place?

"I can't let you do it, Pastor. Not in good conscience."

Rick stepped away from the clump of Sandies—RICK! —and blocked the gurney's path.

Pastor Ed threw up his hands in exasperation. "You would unleash a demon on the world over a woman who's killing herself with alcohol and drugs? Let her go. She wants to go, or she wouldn't drink and do drugs."

"You are casting judgment to rationalize a wrongdoing. Gosh, come on!" Rick turned around, keeping his ass pressed against the gurney as he addressed the sandy-haired trio loitering behind him. "Brothers, please. I won't call you out, but you must come forward with your objections. We all know Jesus taught love and mercy and forgiveness."

In response, shuffling feet, averted gazes, and worshipful glances at their true God, Pastor Ed. Motherfuckers. No wonder Mom fled with her kid. No wonder Amy sequestered with the priests behind stained glass windows. These dudes were the worst.

*Kill them.*

"Shouldn't we be merciful? Shouldn't we rely on faith and love to cast it out?" Rick persisted.

"To where, brother?" Pastor Ed strolled over to him. "Please, enlighten me." Anyone who didn't know better would believe he was an amiable fellow and not in fact closing in on poor Rick. "Where does this abomination go to if we simply 'cast it out'?"

"To hell, right?" Rick turned back to the Sandies.

"Right, brothers?" The words had barely left his mouth before Pastor Ed pushed him straight into the awaiting arms of Gina's hospital guard, who then folded him into a headlock and dragged him into the hallway.

Someone pushed her gurney up alongside an empty coffin. Metallic, same as Dad's. Gina's stomach bounced. This would be how they disposed of her body.

# Chapter Fifty-Two

*Murder them all. Eat their skin. Make ash.*

Pastor Ed kissed the fish charm, then extended his arms out to his sides, ready to speechify. He and Tawny exchanged a glance, after which she clucked and sulked off to sit in the closest pew. This, apparently, was a man's ritual. Doctor Virginia followed her.

Gina's hospital guard returned and nodded at Ed, then took his position next to the other Sandies.

"Brothers. If it gets out of its human vessel, it will resume the hunt." He made eye contact with each of the Sandies. "It will stalk us, stalk our families, stalk our future generations. And as the Rapture approaches, it will join the legions from hell to take this world from Christ, from us, to thrust what was once God's kingdom into chaos and elemental godlessness, where demons reign and the innocent are devoured."

"Amen," said the Sandies.

Virginia, seated next to Tanya, added a "Mm-hm" to hers.

Gina knew little about the Bible, but wouldn't these yo-yos assume they'd be raptured and therefore not be around to fight the demons? Wouldn't they be ensconced in the heavenly kingdom?

Ed raised his hands to the heavens. "In His name, I reclaim any territory given over to Satan and place it in the hands of Jesus Christ. Amen."

The cultists repeated his words.

Except for Rick, who was back, rumpled and bruised and leaning against the frame of the side door with a hand on his ribs. "She's an innocent." His voice was weak. "Please stop. I beg you guys. If not for the salvation of your souls, stop so you don't go to jail."

On a glance from Ed, another Sandy mobilized, lumbering out a different door. He'd come at Rick from behind.

*Do something,*

"God put us on earth to protect innocents from evil," said Pastor Ed. "This is our task, Rick. We save countless others with our act, however terrible. God has sanctified it."

"That's not true. You've made yourself into a false God!"

Tawney made a high-pitched growling noise, but Doctor Virginia wrapped her arms around her. "It's okay, calm down, it's okay."

"Look around a little." Pastor Ed swept his hands out. "We can sanctify the ground, we can cover it in metals, we can seal it with ashes, but someday it will escape confinement. Let's make sure that doesn't happen for a good long time."

"I'm calling the police!" Rick turned and limped off. Poor bastard. Didn't know he was trapped as well.

Ed swayed back and forth. "Lord Jesus Christ, I stand

below Your Cross and beg You to cover me with Your precious blood that pours from Your sacred heart and Your holy wounds. Cleanse us. Cleanse me, my Savior, in the living water flowing from Your heart and surround me with Your Holy Spirit."

Scuffling, nearby.

Rick's voice, begging: "Please, brothers, I'm only—"

Rick yelped. A door slammed.

Together, Gina and her occupier burst from their "inebriation" to scream, *"Ego te furantur pellis!"* (I will eat your skin!)

*Stop. You're making it worse.*

*We kill them all.*

*Escape, not death.*

*Burn. Burn.*

Suspended in an internal battle for primacy, neither Gina nor her occupier noticed Tawny and Virginia mounting the altar stairs, needles in hand, until Ed said, "Let Virginia take care of this, darlin'."

Doctor Virginia approached with the killing syringe. Tawny followed, pouting.

Pastor Ed took hold of Gina's chin. "Please know we do this for God." That motherfucker was weeping. "We do this to protect others!"

*One for many.*

Tawny and Virginia closed in—

—when the *POP-POP* of gunshots interrupted.

## Chapter Fifty-Three

The gun's reports reverberated through the space, leaving in its wake the scent of fireworks.

The Sandies poured back to the altar to shield their pastor from harm, but got only halfway to him when another series rang out, sending everyone ducking or falling to the floor.

*Pop-Pop!*

Amy ascended the altar stairs, dressed in her all-black Sunday best, minus the buggy sunglasses. Her dark eyes held as steady as her gun hand. She aimed both at Pastor Ed.

"You let her go, and she comes with me."

Gina's body juddered as her occupier whisked her back fifty years to the front porch of Dad's house. Gina observed from the awning, spying down at a woman arguing with Young-Amy, who wore long, naturally black hair and a backpack.

". . . if it sees us, Mom! We have to go! Let me bring him with me." Amy stamped her feet. Although unable to hear the exact words, the gist was that Amy could not take the kid. Finally, Amy backed up, and with a forlorn glance at Gina—who realized she was occupying Young-Dad's body —Amy trudged off in defeat.

"Miss Fade, I'm sure you have the best intentions," said Pastor Ed. "Though you know not what you do, my dear lady—"

"Stop your sugary nonsense, Pastor. It might get you a heavy tithing plate, but it does squat for me. I intend to take the girl. We have an appointment with Father Doyle and some holy water."

"You won't kill me, or anybody, Miss Fade. There aren't enough Hail Marys to forgive such a sin."

To that, the Sandies stood up and fanned out to encircle her.

"Yes, I will, for my kin, I will!" She swung the gun back and forth, the steam dissipating with each oscillation. Amy couldn't contend with the hulking towers of beef bearing down on her from all directions. In seconds, they'd plucked the gun from her hand, and the largest fellow carried her kicking and screaming out the front door.

Gina broke. She'd broken before. She'd broken in a pile of her own puke once. She'd broken many times. This was the final breaking. The break with life. How terrible. All she could do was sob for whatever she might have been but never would be.

"Doctor Virginia, you're up," the pastor said.

As the doctor closed in, Gina experienced a Gatling gun series of flashbacks:

—A massive lightning bolt emerged from Dad's mouth, snapping at a screaming woman wearing a bike helmet.

—Fire-vomiting on the drifter.

—A gout of lightning gobbled the unconscious surfer.

—The pastor's sister's body burned to a crisp in a shallow grave.

—From the roof, Dad spat lightning at the barn.

The answer was fire. Of course. Harnessing the flame. She let herself merge with the demon to gather the elements kindling within her, recognizing the same shooting stars she felt in the hospital room. Once joined, the power swelled, popping and crackling, an intense juggernaut awaiting orders. She and her occupier directed this energy to her restraints. Her ankles and wrists grew increasingly hot until blisters threatened.

And then the restraints snapped.

# Chapter Fifty-Four

She sat up, head tilted queerly. Outcries around her.

*Open your mouth!*

Gina obeyed, emitting a mighty roar as the fire streamed out. She hopped off the gurney, a human flamethrower raining hell on the cultists. People rolled around on the altar trying to snuff the flames, their screams muted by the roar of her barrage. Virginia batted at her burning lab coat. Tawny slammed her head into the carpet to snuff the inferno eating her hair.

Pastor Ed eluded the fire on his way to the side door, but Gina spat a stream that nicked his Sunday-best suit jacket and jumped straight up to his pompadour. He screeched as he exited. Whatever hadn't caught him now licked a Jesus-Lion painting before racing up the wall.

Fire wanted out, wanted to play. It used Gina's mouth to roar, "*I am the bringer of death, maker of ashes.*"

All the men, in varying stages of personal destruction, hobbled to the side door. Another dragged the doctor, whose coat had melted into a sticky glaze merged with her skin.

Gina grabbed the gun a Sandy had dropped when assaulted by flames.

She thought about chasing them, shooting them, or incinerating them. No. She'd destroy their clubhouse instead. So, she promenaded down the aisle, pivoting her head like a lawn sprinkler to water the place into a conflagration. During this trip, she struggled to expel her occupier, told it to get out, to stop, to possess a Lamb. It was too strong, too hungry, too busy. And goddamn, this power of extirpation felt divine. Before exiting the vestibule, she sent a ball of fire into a stack of Evangelical Heritage Bibles.

# Chapter Fifty-Five

To her surprise, the power ebbed once she got outside. The thing must have spent its finite amount of energy and would need a brief rest before resuming its path of destruction. She seized the moment and ran to Amy's Lincoln, which idled by the marquee. Amy slumped in the driver's seat looking like someone had flung her inside quickly. Blood trickled from her nostrils.

Dead? Unconscious? What to do here? *Think fast!* A brief debate ensued—

*Discard her.*

*No!*

Gina checked for a pulse, found a weak, fluttering heartbeat. She can't die! She can't die. This was Gina's last relative besides Mom—Mom, whose brain had dimmed enough that she had to be in a care home. Mom, lucid and outstanding during some phone calls and vague in others. She had to get back to Mom, even though Mom was disappearing. And if Mom left, who did she have but this brave and weird old crone?

*Burn her.*

*Fuck you!*

She nudged Amy over to the passenger seat and was about to get in the car when a strange bark behind her heralded the last stand of Tawny, now half-bald with pinwheel eyes.

"I send you to hell! I send you to hell!" she squawked, vocal cords shredded.

An unwilling puppet once again, Gina opened her mouth. This time, instead of fire, she discharged lightning. At the last second, Gina felt her head turn, so it only knocked Tawny senseless.

*Why don't you possess her?*

*I have you.*

*Great. So, I'll kill innocent people and live a wretched life until you destroy me?*

*Fun together.*

*How do I get rid of you?*

An unfamiliar voice in her head said, "*Gina Ballerina, look!*"

It belonged to Dad, who now spirited her to the roof of the house.

"One for many," he said as he lifted his foot.

*One for many,*

Gina stared down at the gun in her hand.

*No!* It shared her thoughts and understood her intentions. *No!*

The church's big window glowed bright with fire rampaging around inside, eating the wood beams and the fancy display Bible.

No time to think. Death was better than possession. Better than a life of constant missteps, of unattainable sobriety, of being so fucking weak. Better than destroying others. No longer broken. Resolute. She had to save the others.

*Do it. Fast. Don't overthink!*

She inserted the cold barrel between her lips. An act as intimate as, but much deadlier than accepting a cigarette. She didn't need anybody to light it for her, though.

# Chapter Fifty-Six

*Don't!*

A ball of magma welled inside her. The occupier wailed.

*I hope there's another life at the end of this. I really do.*

Gina's index finger inched toward the trigger guard.

There would be a second of pain, then nothing. She hoped people wouldn't mistake this for yet another drunkie-junkie checking out because shit got too hard.

*My next life will be better.*

Her finger touched the cold metal of the trigger.

*Momma, you'll join me soon, and you'll recognize my face, and you'll know how to work the toaster and do crafts, and we'll both be happy.*

*Five . . . four . . . three . . . two—*

—magma surged through her, shaking her body like a rag doll. The demon blasted from her mouth as a forked tornado. It vortexed the gun and the church marquee into a twister and flipped Gina onto her back.

The twister spiraled into the inferno and expanded until it was as high and wide as the church itself.

Gina crawled to her feet. Stifled hysterics. What had she almost done?

Was it over?

Self-assessment: the bloat and rage and inner voice were gone. Emptiness never felt so good. She hopped into the car and revved the Lincoln, drowning out the sirens of approaching fire trucks.

The Lincoln had gone five feet when the pastor appeared out of the smoke and threw himself on the hood. His pompadour had incinerated into stubble on a bubbly red scalp. "You murdered my sister!"

*My God, this poor man. He lost his sister. His whole life spent hunting for her murderer.*

Gina zigzagged through the lot until Pastor Ed lost his grip on the windshield wipers and rocketed off, skittering along the pavement like Rick getting road rash as a kid. She'd never forget the sound of the pastor's cries.

A part of her pitied these crazies. They craved church the way she craved inebriation. It blunted the harsh realities of a ghastly, amoral world and provided purpose. Theirs might be the idea of eternal life. Hers had been to submerge herself in a world of patterns and colors without the burden of bad memories. She figured that out in a meeting, and it sounded cooler than saying her world goals had been to find more ways to anesthetize herself against everything.

She idled a moment, waited until the pastor moved. Fucked up, yet alive. Did his eyes glow blue? *No. Not yet at least.*

In minutes, she drove onto Highway 140, headed east.

Would they blame her? If so, they'd have to admit they were planning to sacrifice her. And Amy, if she survived, could confirm. The Lambs' official explanation would have to be "accidental fire."

In her side mirror, smoke rose above the church, morphing into an arrow pointed at her.

# Chapter Fifty-Seven

The speedometer showed her sneaking up on ninety. Shit! If a cop stopped her, the storm would catch up. She eased her foot off the gas until the car coasted down to a safer seventy mph, at which point she set the cruise control.

The arrow had grown to the size of a football field.

*Eyes on the road ahead, not behind. Get to Amy's.*

"Hi."

"Jesus!" She jerked so vehemently that her head hit the headliner. In the rearview mirror, a bruised and battered Rick gave her a meek smile.

He'd pulled a psycho killer move and hidden in the backseat.

"What are you doing?"

"Hitching a ride?"

"Uh-uh. No ride for you."

"Why not?"

"You were the bait!"

"I'm sorry. I didn't know the plan. The *actual* plan."

"You don't honeytrap for a cult and expect absolution."

"I thought we meant well."

"So says every fucking death cult."

"I believed prayer and divine love would—"

"Am I driving in the direction of Auburn?"

"Auburn?"

"Topeka. Am I going the right way?"

"Oh. Yes."

"Shit!"

The firestorm had reshaped into a winged demon, its wings spread wide as it tore across the sky, far faster than seventy mph.

"It's coming too fast!" Gina pressed the accelerator, gaining some distance, though not enough for comfort.

"I assume it's no longer inside you?"

"No, and it's pissed about it."

"Gina, ever since we were kids . . ."

"I'll take you to Auburn, and you can make your way back home. I'd stay away from Ed and the rest if I were you. It must have 'seen' one of them."

Rick sighed. "I sure wish we could start over from that first moment we met, again, on the stairs. Or when we were kids. Gosh, Gina, if you hadn't moved away—"

"Stop already. I don't date dudes who belong to cults. It's my new rule. I mean, sadly, you wouldn't have been my first."

"I don't belong to them anymore."

Her shoulders tightened. *Fuck him and his excuses.* "I don't want to need anybody the way I used to need a drink."

"Okay."

"Belt her in."

Rick leaned over to sit Amy up and affix the seatbelt.

Closer now, this demonic bird of prey shorn of its lightning cloak tracked them, casting the world below it into shadow. All Gina could do was stay strong and keep moving toward the perimeter of its territory, wherever that was.

She switched on the radio. Dwight Yoakam crooned for a few seconds before static took over. She pushed the scan button. Every station crackled with static, and from this static a voice emerged.

*"Gee-nuh!"*

"Shit, what?"

Gina turned off the radio. It popped on again.

Rick gasped.

*"Gee-nuh!"*

"Fuck off." She pressed the button.

"Lord help us," Rick said.

*"I'm comin' for ya, Gee-nuh!"*

She kept her finger on the button, ready for each time the voice returned, refusing to let the bastard slither back into her head.

Now a mere mile behind the Lincoln, Hydra heads flicked forked tongues in tandem with crashing thunder.

If Amy was right, it could only pursue her so far, and it might never reach her, but for now, the monster lingered in her rearview mirror.

Maybe it always would.

The End.

## *Lightning Death Toll*

About 1,500 human beings are struck by lightning in the United States every year, of whom one-third are killed, says Nature Magazine. Nine-tenths of these accidents occur in rural localities.

## Acknowledgments

Thank you Nightmare Press! You have been gracious and kind and helpful. Thanks to two gifted and talented madmen, John Skipp and Garrett Cook for early feedback. Thanks to the amazing Maddy Leary, who did first edits and went above and beyond. A big thank you to my long-gone great grandpa "Poppy," whose boring diary yielded a peculiar newspaper clipping that fascinated me. And thank you, Ron, for always reminding me that I should be writing.

# About the Author

Shelly is a Los Angeles townie who works at a library by day, screenplays and dark fiction by night. Her work has been optioned and/or appeared in a dozen anthologies in the last few years. Ghoulish Books published her debut novel, the sci-fi body horror rom-com, Like Real, in 2023. Laughing Man Press will release her third book, June Bride, in 2027.

As a huge fan of horror made-for-television movies from the sixties through the aughts, she hosts monthly watch parties of such classics as Crowhaven Farm, Yeti: Curse of the Snow Demon, and Satan's School for Girls.

If you wish to meet Shelly in her natural habitat, you'll find her skulking through various Los Angeles neighborhoods in search of a Little Free Library, or standing in line for a double feature at The New Bev.

Find links to her socials at www.shellylyons.com

## More Titles By Nightmare Press!

JOURNEY SLOANE

SURVIVING
UNION
GRACE

The Guardians
Teresa Sewell and Rob Le

VOL. 3
JENNY'S
SPOOKY
LITTLE
TALES:

Coming Soon From Nightmare Press!

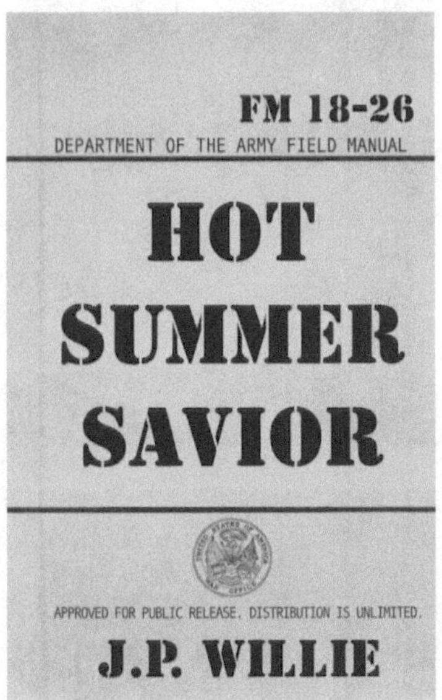

JOSEPH J. BATTAGLIA
THE
CONTINUANCE

MAMA
JOSIE
G.F. MOORE

SNARE FOR A SMALL
ECLIPSE
JASON A. WYCKOFF

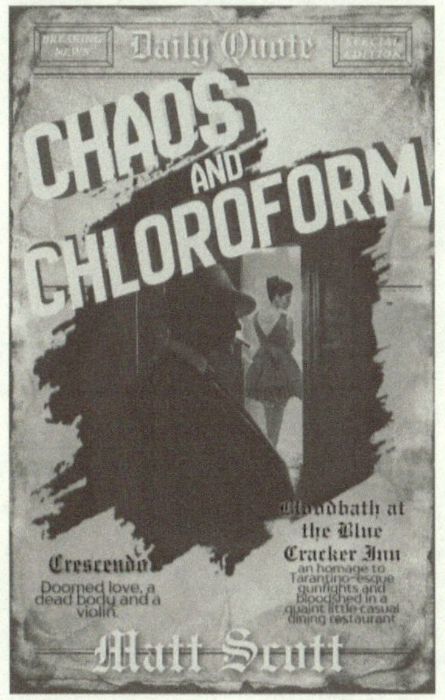
Daily Quote
CHAOS
AND
CHLOROFORM
Bloodbath at the Blue Cracker Inn
an homage to Tarantino-esque gunfights and bloodshed in a quaint little casual dining restaurant
Crescendo
Doomed love, a dead body and a violin.
Matt Scott

www.ingramcontent.com/pod-product-compliance
Lightning Source LLC
LaVergne TN
LVHW041928090826
845145LV00017B/2228

* 9 7 8 1 6 4 9 0 5 0 4 8 9 *